BEYOND CENTAURUS

Crossing the Centaur

by
D.R. Martin

Beyond Centaurus

The Novel

Crossing the Centaur

ISBN-13: 978-0615764818

ISBN-10: 0615764819

Thorfinnsson Publishing

Warrenville, IL USA

Dedicated to my wife, Karen.

I would be lost without you.

Beings, Places & Things

(In alphabetical order by first name)

Anna Stotfold

Mars Polar Base Director

-

Battle Computer

Tactical computer worn on the wrist, capable of detecting and analyzing radiation, environment, materials, and more

-

Bruce Tupou Jones

Survivor on the Island of Tonga

-

D'gotari

Alien species that strongly resembles the "Greys" from old Earth UFO reports

Emily Glass

Ship's Captain, Radian

-

George Olafson

Ship's Engineer, Glasgow

-

Herbert Pickard

Systems Engineer/Passenger, Radian

-

Izar

World where the nano technology was stolen

-

Kai

Survivor on the Island of Tonga

Kvaaa'tu

Vajhi historian and archeologist

-

Kree

A race renowned for commercial shipbuilding on the Frontier

-

The Lebrith

One of the thirteen Ancient Races

-

Lobruc

Bounty Hunter from Sooggao Uxi

-

Captain Mitchell

Late Ship's Captain, Sargasso

Perseus Cole

Ship's Captain, Glasgow

-

Prdynon

A nomad insectoid race

-

Pycari

Izari Scientist

-

Quinzea

The planet hosting the Frontier Free Trade Zone known as The Thieves Market

-

Rachael Yin

Communications Officer, Glasgow

Robert MacKesson

Colonel, Special Services, Class IX Field Agent

-

Virtual Interface

Linked to the battle computer, the VI uses micro-lasers implanted in the eye socket to paint the computer display directly on the retina. This allows the user to access data covertly

-

Voefsee Idi

Prdynon friend of Wenvin Wo who lives on Izar

-

Wenvin Azivdeo

Prdynon shopkeeper and counselor to Wenvin Wo

-

Wenvin Wo

Prdynon Insectoid/Specialty Thief for Hire

Wesley Greyson

Supply Officer Sargasso/Operations, Luna Base

-

Yuud Masar

Xihji Trademaster

-

Zigs

Slang term for the Zone Guard in the Quinzean Free Trade Zone

Prologue

It is the stars. When I'm staring into the stars time becomes meaningless. The past and the present become one. The past. Therein lays the problem. It's a tough galaxy. Money makes everything move, and out here where sunlight never touches, money is at the heart of every action. Once you have figured this out, anticipating the actions of others becomes second nature. Usually. When dealing with aliens, especially those new to the frontier it's always best to assume the worst.

The alien sitting across from me wasn't new. He was from a race of intellectuals. Apparently, his species evolved on a planet of exclusively herbivores. Without ever experiencing predation throughout their ancestries, they evolved with little to no innate aggression. They almost function as a collective in their society. Kvaaa'tu was what we would call an archaeologist. He was from a world orbiting a star in the inner galaxy that was unknown to Earth. Its name is unpronounceable in English; however, a merchant had earlier referred to them as the Vajhi. That translated. The Difficult Ones.

*****

The lilting, musical tones of Kvaaa'tu's voice drifted through the air. The translator hesitated while its processor light flickered away. Kvaaa'tu's language was insanely complicated. Every word has an exclusive and specific meaning. There are no words with double meanings. No one really knows how many words are in their language, as new terms are created everyday as discoveries are made. I had heard of simple treaties with them, which translated to over ten million words.

Finally, the translator crackled to life, "Does MacKesson intend to engage in data exchange proposed by Kvaaa'tu?"

He tracked me down after hearing that there was a sole human living alone in the Frontier. He was documenting the history of another race that had appeared on the galactic scene out of nowhere and disappeared just as quickly. That race was man.

Humans entered the frontier with the same arrogance with which we marched across Earth conquering every species in our path. We were in for a shock. The races of the Frontier had seen the same types come and go for thousands of millennia. The ones who learned quickly remained. Some withdrew to their home worlds to stay, and sadly, many perished. Earlier, Kvaaa'tu had explained to me in long and precise detail that he was tasked to detail the history of these worlds.

The older races have learned that nature has checks and balances. When anything becomes unbalanced, be it in power or wealth, an infinite universe always has a negating factor. Some other planet, alliance, faction, or even natural disaster itself, is waiting in the shadows to correct the imbalance.

Equilibrium is necessary anywhere thousands of races interact. Conflict is inevitable, and frontier justice is swift. As long as the balance is undisturbed, conflicts rarely spread, and overall peace is maintained.

It took us too long to learn to not rock the boat.

I returned my gaze to Kvaaa'tu and said, "I am willing to help you. What do you offer in trade?"

The processor light returned to a flurry of activity. On the Frontier, anything of value is traded. Value is exchanged for value. Credit and debt are rare. One reason for this is that it isn't uncommon for any given time to be the last time you see someone. It's a cold galaxy and the death of an individual, or the extinction of a race is rarely noticed beyond the ledger of some trader.

The translator had exchanged lyrical tones with my companion and voiced its translation, "Accepted. I offer detailed physical, orbital, tectonic, climate, and positional data for this quadrant of this galaxy. Indicate if you accept."

It sounded like he was offering me one of the oldest trading items, maps. His race was renowned for their galactic charts.

"You've got a deal," I said.

The translator made an unpleasant noise then announced, "Submission too vague. Please restate."

I wouldn't want to marry a Vajhi woman, I sighed to myself, "Offer accepted.   Verbal data transfer ready to begin."

Thankfully, I didn't have to tell him my story in this way. They digitally image the storyteller as the narrative is told, recording every nuance of body language,   facial   expressions,   and   bio   signs. Additionally, the native language sample is archived as well. They can then pick the recordings apart at their leisure.

I sat back and began.

"It has been ten Earth years since I left my home star system…

I

Arrogance, Thy Name is Man

Earth had only been a space fairing culture for one hundred and fifty years when an accident at a micro black hole research facility generated a space-time shock wave, which attracted the attention of a curious alien vessel who happened to be passing only a few light-years away.

The accident had destroyed Europa. Most of the personnel made it off the station before the planet-sized moon had been torn to bits. Now the orbit of Jupiter was as dangerous from Europa's debris as the orbit of Earth from satellite debris of the twenty first century.

Europa Trans-Light Research Station had been placed in a remote location due to extreme danger in experimenting with artificial black holes. While the Europa project didn't directly achieve their goal, the fortunate encounter with a non-hostile race propelled mankind into interstellar space.

They were a ship of traders. Six different species. Earth welcomed them warmly. Trades were negotiated, gifts given. When the circus was over Earth was minus some archeological treasures, but the proud owners of gravity drive technology.

That was over a century ago. It took another twenty five years to adapt the technology for deep space expeditions.

Then man found the Frontier. The Frontier was the closest English translation for the thirty thousand light-year stretch of space that from Earth appears in the Centaurus constellation of the Milky Way. It's a free trade zone encompassing tens of thousands of worlds.

With interstellar travel and translation technology at our disposal, it only took another five years to be at war over a trade dispute. Records from that period are scant. In less than one week, the forces of Earth were annihilated. Mankind never recovered. Less than one hundred thousand survived on Earth, from a population of nearly six billion. The off-world colonies were wiped out.

Once their domes were penetrated, and ships disabled, any hopes for survival vanished with their precious air that rushed into space.

I was there.

In 2084, I was assigned to monitor security at a nanotechnology facility under the icecap at Mars' South Pole. Officially, their project involved developing nanobots, which could allow humans to survive on the surface of Mars without environmental suits.

The technology to work at the atomic scale had been acquired through some shady dealings by Extra-planetary Affairs. This, I know, because I negotiated for EA. EA was the "independent" agency appointed by the six nations of Earth. Independent to the extent that every controlling officer was selected by IP, the Mega Corporation which held the monopoly on space travel. IP stood for Infinite Possibilities. I had been a prime candidate for company service. They preferred contracting retired military officers, and I had made a career as a Special Services Field Agent in the Unification Wars of the late 21st century.

Two decades of global war on Earth had ended with the formation of the Six Nations of Earth. This was due in no small part to the fact that the war had nearly bankrupted the planet with the exception of the weapons industry, which then made the simple transition into space travel.

During the war, Special Services operatives were trained to do the nasty little jobs, which no one ever finds out about. When a diplomat met with an accident, it was usually no accident. Accomplish your objective. Period. That's what the Special Services drilled into you, and what IP considered to be a valuable trait. They held so much influence, that official reassignment as an 'Independent Field Agent' was assured if IP wanted you. The company can be good to those with valuable traits. However, no matter how much wealth you acquire, sometimes the stars have different ideas about your future.

*****

Twenty-four Hours before the attack

"MacKesson, Robert," I said as I handed my identity chip to the Mars colony admissions officer.

"Do you have any negotiables, consumables, or gifts worth more than fifty credits?" she asked as she slipped my chip into the computer.

The screen flashed and a soft tone sounded. "Oh! Diplomatic credentials, I see..." the officer remarked, half to herself. "Go right on through, sir."

I gave her a tight smile as she handed me my ID chip, and moved on.

I tapped my communicator and said, "This is MacKesson. I have arrived."

"Robert MacKesson confirmed. Welcome to Mars. Your escort is waiting at airlock four, ready for priority departure." a soothing, though not quite human voice replied.

"Understood. Airlock four. If you could direct me..." I said.

"One hundred and fifty meters to your right to the dome, then turn left for fifty meters," the voice replied.

I glanced down the dimly lit street and hit transmit, "Acknowledged. En-route."

The computer would ignore this reply, I knew, but it was hard not to treat it as human at times.

It was much darker in the dome than I was accustomed to. Even though it was transparent, the weak sunlight low on the pink horizon did little to illuminate the streets. Power was always at a premium in an ever-expanding colony, and streetlights weren't a priority. Most of the structures looked to be fashioned from some type of adobe. It all had the same red hue as the Martian surface. As my eyes adjusted to the lower light levels, I began to notice a kind of haze in the air. Something burning I suspected. At the dome, I paused for a few seconds. No matter how many times I look out over Mars I never cease to be transfixed by the rugged beauty. I picked up my bag and turned toward the airlock, enjoying the feeling of only weighing a little over a third of normal.

As I approached the airlock four facility, a hulking form stepped out of the door and snaps to attention, "I'm Sargent Harris. This way, Sir."

"That's a nice piece of hardware you have there..." I said, gesturing to the fleet assault weapon hanging at his side. "Expecting trouble?"

"Standard procedure for ultra-secure facilities, sir." he rumbled.

We sped through to a light air transport, which was waiting inside the airlock. In seconds, we were inside and the outer door was closed. There was a mild shutter inside the transport as the outside pressure dropped suddenly. They hadn't waited to depressurize, they had just opened the outer door. We were in some hurry.

I turned to Harris, "What's with the evac style exit? Is there a problem at the lab?"

He glanced over his shoulder at me and said "Weather. There's a massive sandstorm building in the southern hemisphere. If we don't get to the base before our window closes we could be stuck for months!"

"I see!" I replied. "How long till we arrive?"

"About an hour. Your briefing is on the computer." Harris said in a tone that made it clear he wasn't interested in conversation.

I turned my attention to the briefing files. As I wasn't sure what clearance Harris held, I decided to use my Virtual Interface to view the files. The VI was a rather useful implant that I acquired during service. An image of the files appeared hovering in the air in front of my eye. In reality, it was being painted on my retina via micro laser. It was all controlled with the battle computer I wore on my wrist.

I was interested to read about the project. The security level said there was more to it than just being able to go outside the domes.

I opened the file, and was not disappointed. The nanotechnology I acquired had obviously been coupled with alien technology from another source, for this was far beyond Earth's knowledge. A self-replicating nanobot, built on the atomic scale. Capable of directly manipulating, and even altering molecules. The possibilities were endless. So was its potential for misuse. Once the molecular manipulation was mastered, researchers were trying to program the nano's quantum computers Artificial Intelligence with a map of the genome of the individual. From that, the nano's could counteract most cell damage at the molecular level. This could easily conquer aging and disease, but just as easily be programmed to destroy. A programmable, smart virus. A more frightening prospect than this hadn't come along in a few years. Nothing is quite as innovative as man's talent for creating new ways to destroy himself, deliberately or accidentally. Someone high up must have realized the potential of this. That would explain why the company would send a field agent on an internal matter. We usually only handled off the book 'negotiations'. Dealing with a bunch of scientists was going to be taxing on my patience I expected.

In a few minutes, we would be touching down. I really wanted to know how far this project had advanced. It all seemed impossible, but my job wasn't to say what was or wasn't possible. My job was to make sure no data left the base in any form. Uncover any leaks, recover the data, and eliminate the mole. If the only way in or out was flying halfway across the planet, it should be relatively easy to nail down anyone who had ever been there. It wasn't like there were many tourists wandering the Martian surface in the sub-zero, toxic atmosphere.

The engine pitch got shrill, and I felt the tug of Earth G+ gravity for a few seconds as we swooped into the gantry. I stiffened involuntarily as we appeared to be headed into a canyon wall. As we approached, a huge rust colored door dropped to expose a large landing bay. As we followed the guide lights to our berth, I could see suited figures working on a squadron of Scorpion fighters. I was unaware the military presence here was quite so large. It was reassuring, in case I met strong resistance from the natives.

There was a strong hum and scraping sound as the magnetic guides pulled us into the docking clamps. A jolt and a hiss later the door was open.

Harris turned and said, "Here ya go. Control knows we're here. Someone will be waiting outside the airlock. Sorry for the silent treatment. Orders"

That statement stuck in my mind. Did he mean standard security 'no extraneous conversation' or was he trying to tell me someone was already covering something up? The airlock closed behind me as the bio-filters clicked and hissed. In a few seconds, the outer door opened. I cautiously stepped through still not quite used to the gravity.

A tall woman stood in the hallway with an air of authority. "Mr. MacKesson, I am Facilities Director Anna Stotfold," she said offering her hand.

"Call me Mac." I replied, startled at the strong grip.

She smiled and said, "And you can call me Anna. We're informal for the most part. If you will follow me to my office, we can get right to work."

25

"Lead the way," I said as we started down the corridor.

The entire facility seemed to be built right into the bedrock under the icecap. With the entrance well below the surface in a canyon carved eons ago when water flowed on Mars' surface. Easily defensible and well off the radar. After twisting through a maze of corridors, we entered a large sparsely deteriorated office.

"Have a seat," Anna said, gesturing toward a pair of high backed leather chairs parted by a small table holding a decanter and glasses. "Would you like a drink?"

"Yes, thanks," I said as I sat down, "So what has happened to warrant this visit?"

The Director looked startled for an instant, and then smiled. "You don't beat around the bush! I like that!"

"I rarely have the luxury of being able to acknowledge pleasantries. I wouldn't have been sent here unless someone high up was nervous," I said.

Her expression deadened. "More than nervous. Now that you're here, there's no reason not to give you the real story. "

"The report did leave a lot of blanks," I said.

"So far, this base and the Six Nations Council are the only ones who know what I am about to tell you. As you may have guessed this facility is for more than researching ways to live on Mars. While this was one of the initial goals, a new threat has emerged and we need to bring every conceivable weapon to bear. A conflict has broken out between an Earth trading outfit and some aliens. We don't know what happened exactly, but it ended in an Earth ship firing on, and nearly destroying a colony in the Izar system. In hours, a single ship from their home world had obliterated the battleship Caucasus and three escort ships. Despite the best diplomatic efforts of the Council, the Izars refuse all attempts at defusing this situation. War is coming. This time with a foe who's as far ahead of us technologically as the Europeans were ahead of the Native Americans." Anna explained.

I emerged from my stunned silence, "From what I read in the report, your project could be turned into one lethal bio-weapon."

"Not in this case," She replied. "In order to have a specific bio-weapon we must have a sample of the genetic material of the target species. If we targeted some particular bio-function with them it could spread to unintended species, even us."

Anna walked over and sat beside me. I took the glass she offered me and sipped. Bourbon. Not top shelf, but good for Mars. "Can we get some of their DNA from contact sources?" I queried.

She gave me a grim look over her glass. "Since the colony was destroyed, every human in that sector has been killed. We're going to be destroyed and we will never even know why."

"So what can nanos do against an alien armada with enough firepower to destroy a Phoenix class Battleship?" I asked.

"Since we don't have Izar DNA to work with, we used what we had available. Human." She explained.

"I don't follow."

"Information acquired from some Arcturan traders led the Council to believe the Izars are massing ships to attack Earth. They know that our military is no match for the Izars. If we send ships to engage the enemy, we send them to certain death. The Council believes man's only hope may be guerrilla resistance. While their starships can destroy the cities from orbit, the Council is gambling on the hope that they will not be willing to stage a landing and invasion. Moreover, if they do, they want our troops to have every advantage we can give them. Imagine a soldier with a team of medics flowing through every cell in his body. They can enhance his vision, increase his strength, convert poisonous gases into oxygen... In short, create a soldier who can fight for weeks without getting tired, without needing sleep. This could be the key to keeping the human race alive." She explained.

I sat back for a moment, and then asked, "So what is it that you need of me? It doesn't seem likely that any Izar spies could have infiltrated."

She shook her head. "No, it's not that. The Council doesn't want knowledge of this attack to be made public until preparations have been made to relocate the people away from the cities. If there is a panic, millions could be killed. Our cover story had to be leaked out to explain our presence here. Too much secrecy paints a big target on your back. However, there was an unexpected downside. We have a mole in the facility. Not Izar, but a corporate spy trying to abscond with the new nano technology. We only got wind of it 4 days ago. The mole's handler has been arrested, and their communicator was seized before anything was compromised. However, we still do not know who the mole is. We have to find this bastard and make sure none of what he might know ever leaves this place."

"Any chance of using the communicator to draw out the mole?" I asked.

Anna shook her head. "Not likely. They don't know if there were any code words used to authenticate their identities, a common practice. Plus," she added, "They probably know that they have been made from the lack of contact with their handler."

"What about the handler?" I asked.

She shook her head, "No, the handler was a mule. He wore a camera, which scrambled and retransmitted the mole's report to someone within a few miles. It wasn't bi-directional communication, so they had no way to track the signal to the receiver."

I gestured around. "How deep is this place?"

"One hundred and fifty meters beneath the surface at the shallowest point. *Five* hundred to the bottom level," She emphasized.

"So no danger of personal satellite transmitters. What are the normal communication channels?" I queried.

31

"All information entering or leaving this facility must pass through my terminal then through a maximum security direct connection to the Council's Critical Control Room. Every message is analyzed for hidden content. There is no way they could have contacts in Critical Control, for they already know what we know," she said confidently.

"So the only way to get a message out of this place is to go outside and send a radio signal which would be picked up instantly, or smuggle a message out to the colony through the supply chain," I thought aloud.

"So it would seem," she said, "but that would require another person in the know, and that person would have to be a regular on the supply runs, which are assigned at random. No waste leaves here. It is all incinerated."

I nodded, "I would like to take a shower and change if possible. I have been too long on vessels with poor ventilation and limited water on this trip." I said as I stood up.

"Certainly. I will have someone show you to your quarters," she said as she reached for her com link.

II

You Can't Hide Under Ground

The next morning began abruptly with an alarm call from the computer. There was just something about the new voice that the Company was using these days. Too soothing and calm. While a panicked sounding computer wouldn't be very useful, this one sounded like it was forever drowsy.

I selected a food pack from the dispenser and sat down to go over the technical drawings of the facility. It was a big place to be focused on something so small. The three dimensional image looked like some bizarre termite mound with tunnels leading off in every direction to rooms of various sizes. Everything was very departmentalized with different sections completely disconnected. I was unsure if this was due to some volatile aspect of the project or simply for information control. The place was powered by a fusion reactor power pack, located in the bottom level. They had obviously not wanted to run out of power.

"Computer, location. Facilities Director?" I queried.

"Director Stotfold is in Microscopy" the machine replied.

I quickly downloaded the station information into my wrist link so that I could pull it up on the VI on demand. I checked my weapon's charge and slid it into a slim holster in the small of my back. Overt arms seemed to make science types nervous, and would put them on their guard. I still had an old slug thrower that I had inherited from my grandfather who served as a Colonel for the United States up until he retired in 2052. It was a .380 caliber Walther PPK that he had purchased as an antique after seeing it in some vintage movies. He always told me that it never hurts to have a weapon that isn't reliant on a power cell. I smiled as I returned it to its usual place secured to my ankle.

I secured my room and headed off down the corridor with the floor plan of the base hovering invisibly in front of me.

35

The design of the base was in a large descending spiral. A design made efficient by Mars' low gravity. Walking uphill is pretty easy when you weigh less than half-normal. Off this spiral corridor snaked side tunnels leading to the various laboratories, offices, and personal quarters.

Five minutes later, I turned down an arched hallway bearing the Microscopy symbol. The hallway opened into a huge chamber carved into the Mars bedrock. There were a number of people busily working at computer consoles.

I stopped a young man who was rushing by. "Where can I find Ms. Stotfold?" I asked.

He pointed across the chamber to a catwalk on the side of a huge machine.

"There." he said as he hurried on about his business.

I walked over and climbed up. There was an access panel leaning against the railing and two behinds protruding from the panel's normal place. I could hear their voices echoing hollowly inside.

"Excuse me," I said getting no reply. "Hello?" I said again as I tapped the panel against the railing.

Anna Stotfold's dark hair emerged from the machine with a screwdriver in her mouth and an optical circuit analyzer in her hand. "Sorry," she said as she dropped the screwdriver, "I was trying to help trace a fault. The bad thing about being on the cutting edge of tech is there are no manuals or repair procedures for a machine that didn't exist a year ago."

"I am sure! I don't envy your job!" I said as she took off her coveralls. "I will try not to interfere with the work more than is absolutely necessary."

She chuckled "With some of them you may have a hard time getting them to notice you're there! Their work is their passion. Some can get quite hostile when distracted."

I smiled at the thoughts of hostility from some of these people. Looking around it didn't appear anyone was capable of throwing a good hissy fit, much less posing a problem.

Anna turned and slid lightly down the ladder. "Come on," she said, "let me give you the VIP tour!"

"I'm right behind you!"

"We'll start with where we are. This is where the nanos are pulled apart for inspection after they are made. They are made by other nanos. In the beginning, we had to create a nanobot that was nothing more than a remote controlled construction droid. With that, we built simple AI nanos to build smarter nanos. Now we are at the stage where we design and they build without our help. Samples come here to make sure that everything is according to design specifications," she said.

"Wow!" I said. "I hope they don't decide that we're no longer the bosses!"

Anna laughed. "Not likely. It is quite a trick to get even the simplest artificial intelligence algorithm into something the size of a virus! Using a form of replicator technology, they can create tools to do their jobs, as they are needed. They are powered by thermal conversion. Run right off your body heat. Follow me and I'll show you the factory."

We walked back out to the spiral and descended three more levels with the Director pointing out various departments as we passed them. Shortly we entered a much smaller chamber than the Microscopy department, simply labeled 'Production'. The walls were lined with computer terminals that formed arcs on either side of two tall electronics towers supporting between them what appeared to be a glass tank.

"This… is our factory," she said gesturing toward the tank.

I stepped closer. It appeared to be filled with a metallic liquid. I wasn't quite sure what I was seeing. "This is the raw material?"

Anna shook her head. "This is what trillions of nanos building trillions of nanos looks like! We have twelve full levels of computers just to coordinate and communicate with them."

It was hard to hide my surprise at what I was seeing. "When you said you were going to show me the factory I was expecting... well, more!"

She laughed again "Yes, but it is literally the production floor!"

A sharp tone sounded from her wrist link and she turned away. I was still fascinated by what I was seeing. Now that I was up close, it was almost as if I could see the shimmers and sparkles of the nanos busy about their work.

Anna Stotfold turned back to me with an ashen expression. "I have to get to C&C. Mr. MacKesson, you had better come too," she said as she sprinted down the corridor toward the Spiral.

I followed quickly behind her wondering what had happened. When we entered Command & Control, it was obvious that everyone on duty was shaken.

I took Anna by the arm, "What's going on?"

"It's started I think," she said turning toward a young woman wearing an earpiece. "Robbie, are you sure it isn't a satellite failure?"

"No, Ma'am. I'm getting a diagnostic feed from it. We aren't getting any response from the outer colonies. I heard distress signals, but only for a moment then they went dead!" the radio operator answered.

"Source?" Anna demanded.

"There wasn't time to lock in."

"How long since we've heard from Earth?"

"Three hours, sir!" a voice replied. "Sir! We're reading seismic activity!"

Seismic activity on Mars could only mean one thing. Impact. Whether from meteorite or bombardment, sound travels well through Mars' rocky core.

"Can you display the seismic reading and triangulate?" I said.

A large display showed the sweeps of an earthquake. I had seen this before during a lunar bombardment during the war.

"Where is it?" I shouted.

41

"Oh my God! It's right under the colony!" Anna gasped as an image of Mars flashed up on the screen.

"We're under attack! I wonder if they know about us," I pondered aloud. "Director, you should evacuate all of your people to the lower levels. Is there an evac plan?"

She turned and looked at me. "No. We are so deep that it was thought nothing could reach us, and so remote there's nowhere to evac to. We're under one hundred and fifty meters of rock then another three hundred of ice. What could penetrate that?"

I gestured toward the data display. "Look at the intensity of those waves. They are getting pounded out of existence. Our best battleship couldn't shake the planet like that. If they can figure out exactly where we are they just might have the power to reach us."

Suddenly, the room fell silent as the alarm silenced and the line went flat. Moments later we all felt a shudder pass through the stone walls around us, and klaxons sounded throughout the base. This time the display was showing a much stronger signal.

"It's centered on the Gamma Nine mining station," a voice shouted from the other side of the room.

The alert lights glinted in Anna's eyes. "They are only three hundred kilometers away."

I tapped a command into my wrist link and the base layout appeared in front of my eye. "Warehouse area seven is the deepest and farthest from the central core. Your inventory says the food stores are near there as well. Order an evacuation to that area. How many people do you have?"

"Two hundred and seventy-nine personnel total." she said as she opened the PA channel to give the order.

I turned to the room and said "Everyone secure your station and move to Warehouse area seven. Now!"

The vibrations suddenly stopped. Everyone paused and looked at each other almost in a trance-like state.

"Move Goddammit! We're next!" I roared shoving the nearest body toward the door. From the few minutes it took for the attack to move from Alpha colony to the mining station I figured this was all being done from orbit. That means we only had minutes or seconds. We cleared the corridor and began the mad dash down the Spiral to our refuge. Before we had made it, a full level the floor seemed to drop away from our feet then spring back, sending everyone crashing to their knees. A deafening roar began to emanate from all around us as the bedrock absorbed unimaginable amounts of energy.

"Keep going! Get to the warehouse!" I shouted in vain against the thunderous noise.

Anna waved to me as she struggled to get to her feet. I made my way over to her and tried to get her to her feet. The motion was like a constant eight-point earthquake and it made standing a challenge.

She pulled me down beside her and yelled in my ear, "You have to get them to Earth!" and in a quick movement she pressed a hypo spray against my neck.

I felt the sharp sting of the injection before I had a chance to react.

"What did you just do to me?" I opened my mouth to yell, but the air rushed from my lungs as a violent wind ripped through the corridor. The structure had been breached. As the rocks began to fall around us I wondered if they would even bother landing to inspect their handy work. There was a loud cracking noise and the floor fell away from us.

III

Awakening

It was dark. Cold. Cold like I had only felt once before during deep space emergency decompression training.

I cautiously tried to move. Nothing seemed to be broken. I tapped my wrist link and it's pale blue glow told me I wasn't dead. I activated the light on the useful little device and took a look around my surroundings.

I seemed to have fallen into a fissure opened by the attack. I powered up my virtual interface and checked the environmental sensors. I couldn't believe what they were showing. I was not only alive, but conscious in Mars' atmosphere!

Suddenly I remembered the last moments before I blacked out as the Spiral collapsed around us. The desperate request of... Anna.

I shined my light around again and saw a couple of shapes near the end of the fissure. I slowly stood and walked over to the lifeless forms. I recognized one. The girl called Robbie from C&C. I closed her sightless eyes and moved away.

The sharp sting before everything went black... That must have been the nanos Anna injected me with. It was the only explanation for me still being alive. I had read up on them last night, and the plan was that the nanos would remove the carbon from the CO_2, and split the oxygen molecules apart. Resulting in oxygen for the host, and carbon to build another nano. At least that part of them seemed to work.

The task at hand seemed to be simple. I could do nothing from where I was so escape was first priority.

I followed the fissure for what seemed like miles. A few more unfortunate scientists had fallen into this fissure as well. Eventually I came to the end.

I could see a glimmer of light coming from about ten meters above me. A quick inspection found a spot there the fissure was narrow enough to climb.

In the light gravity, I almost felt as if I could simply climb the wall hand over hand. I made it to the light source and climbed out of a crack in the canyon wall onto the canyon floor. I guess I was the first and only person to ever get trapped on the Martian surface unprotected and survive.

From the bottom of the canyon, I could tell that it was daylight, but not the location of the sun. I approached the canyon wall with the same method I had used for years on Earth. However, it turned out to be rather awkward in the low gravity. I found I could easily support my weight with one hand on almost any stone protuberance. I climbed the canyon walls faster than seemed possible. I was beginning to wonder what else these nanos were programmed to do.

When I reached the top of the canyon, I paused to take in the surroundings. The canyon I was in wasn't a canyon, but another fissure.

I had emerged on the rim of what was left of the polar base. The ice had retreated a kilometer from the impact point. The center of the crater appeared to have been liquefied. I couldn't imagine what it took to do this.

I pulled up everything I had about Mars to try to find some means of transportation. After a few moments, I found references to prospector drones, which had been used in the early days of exploration of Mars.

Their mission had been to locate mineral deposits and return ore samples to Earth. There was supposed to be twenty or more prospectors somewhere on the planet. Nevertheless, due to their autonomous design, only one recently recorded location. It had been spotted by a survey team at Sulci Gordii near the base of Olympus Mons... A quarter of the way around the planet. I tapped my wrist link and pulled up a map of Mars. Six thousand, two hundred and fifty-four kilometers. I was going to have to find some resources if I hoped to survive. Even with the help of the nanos, walking that far without food and water would be impossible. Then I remembered the shuttle bay in the cliff side. It was a long way from the central core of the base. If the aliens were targeting the reactor, then the shuttle bay might have escaped destruction.

I highlighted the hangar on the map and locked in the coordinates. I glanced skyward at the rapidly advancing sun. If I didn't make it to the shuttle bay before sundown, I'd be faced with spending the night exposed to the Martian night. I began to run in the direction of the indicator floating in my eye. I was beginning to get used to the lighter gravity and made good time to the edge of the cliff. According to my wrist link, I was right above the entrance. Two hundred meters above. From my perspective, I could only see the chasm dropping away in front of me. Descending without rappelling gear is always more intimidating than climbing. I took a deep breath and swung my legs over the precipice. The fractured surface offered plentiful handholds for the low gravity climb down, and before long, I dropped into the mouth of the shuttle bay.

I made my way along the dark bay led by the small pool of light offered by my wrist link torch. About one hundred meters in I came to the airlock. It was still intact, but there was no power. I opened the override panel and released the interlock, then inserted a crank into an access port and slowly wound the door open. The inner door stood open. I could see several frozen bodies in the control room. I followed the corridor toward the main complex in the vain hope of finding someone alive but the tunnel was collapsed a short way past the shuttle bay section. I returned to the control room and began to search for anything useful.

In a group of lockers was complete surface turnout gear. I quickly put on a set and turned on the helmet floodlight. The nanos may have somehow kept me from freezing physically, but the cold was just as real to me.

Planetary environment suits were different from space suits. These were closer akin to an old-fashioned cold-water diver neoprene suit. Rather than using a petroleum-based material for insulation, they used vacuum micro-cell. It mimics a vacuum cylinder. It's remarkable insulation properties allowed the suit to be only six millimeters thick but still keep a human alive to minus one hundred centigrade. The tension of the tight suit replaced the pressurized suits of old. You still had a heated helmet and the oxygen generator to contend with but otherwise movement was unrestricted.

Now that I was getting warmed up a bit, I sat down to have something to eat and to work out my next move. According to my wrist link, it had been a day and a half since the attack. That must have meant I had been unconscious for twenty-four hours or more. I guess the nanos didn't have much time to prepare for all hell breaking loose. Get them to Earth. That was the last thing Anna said. I looked skyward and wondered for a moment how Earth was faring against the alien bombardment. Earth defenses were formidable with planetary power reserves.

A long search of the accessible areas turned up nothing of any immediate use. The Scorpion fighters had obviously been dispatched to their untimely end. An abandoned tool kit lying open in place since the attack offered me a good starting point for some makeshift survival gear. I discarded anything not likely to be helpful and filled the bag with emergency rations and frozen water packs. I paused as I passed a corpse slumped over a terminal. I noticed a radio on his side. I took it and looked at the charge. Dead. I quickly backtracked to the equipment room I had passed earlier. I was in luck. There were power packs there. I ejected the radios power cell and slotted a new one in its place. The display glowed with life. Unfortunately, this radio was on a short-range frequency. However, if a ship were nearly overhead in low orbit and were monitoring a short-range frequency, I might be heard. A lot of ifs, but nothing more promising had turned up.

"Hello? Is there anyone receiving me?" I said as I held the transmit button. Silence filled the room. "This is Colonel Robert MacKesson to anyone who can hear this transmission... Please respond."

Again, silence. If there was anyone else alive in this complex, they couldn't hear, or couldn't respond.

I pulled my survival kit onto my back and started back to the landing bay. Just before the airlock, I noticed a door that I had missed on the way in. I opened it to reveal a spiral staircase winding downward. I followed it for what seemed like an impossibly long time, wondering where I was going. Just as I was considering turning back, there was a distinct change in the echo of my steps. A few more twists brought me to another door. Shoving it open, I saw another entry bay. Looking out the window, I could dimly see a surface vehicle. I opened the airlock doors and walked in to get a closer look. It was one of the old style short-range rovers. I tossed my pack onto the open seat and went to the maintenance area off to the side to grab a fuel cell and connect it to the rover. The touch of a switch brought the displays to life. Another tap and the bay was flooded with light. I quickly loaded all of the spare power cells into the back of the rover. I didn't know what the range was of these things, but I was fairly certain it wasn't six thousand kilometers. I climbed into the driver's seat and spun the six-wheeled beast around in its tracks illuminating the external door a few meters down the tunnel. I pulled forward then climbed out to crank the door open.

IV

A Perilous Drive

The reddish light reflected off of the high canyon walls illuminated a well-worn path out into the canyon. I drove forward with the high-pitched whine of the rover's motors, and the crunching regolith under the wheels the only sound.

My wrist-link could tell me distance and bearing to the mining unit's last location, but it couldn't tell me how to get there.

There were no surface roads on Mars. I hoped that following the worn path would get me out of the canyon. It would seem pointless to put a surface access in a location where you couldn't access the surface.

I glanced back over the base layout map. The surface exit was not on it, so any hope of finding an attached surface map vanished.

Luckily, it was summer for this pole now, so the days were long. Trying to navigate a jagged, rutted landscape with nothing but headlights would be very difficult.

The path wound along the bottom of the canyon until it was suddenly blocked by a slope of debris. Here the canyon was only about fifty meters deep, and the path wound up the side of the debris flow.

A few more moments and I crested the rim of what turned out to be a crater about a kilometer across. I followed the rim around to emerge on the plain.

I locked in on the mining site at Olympus Mons and turned the rover to follow the little red arrow hovering invisibly in front of my eye.

Now that I had a clear view of the horizon, I could see the dust storm that Harris had mentioned on our flight in. It seemed to be inching it's way in my direction. I decided to shift my bearing far enough to make sure I skirted the storm. I had read enough to know that the five hundred-kph winds would sandblast anything on the surface out of existence. Even if the nanos could somehow protect me, which I doubted, the rover would be toast. Better to try to avoid that at all costs.

I drove across the barren plain in a futile chase of the horizon. The storm had moved off to the southeast, and I hoped to be well clear of its next pass if this one made it around the planet again.

As I moved northward, night began to return. The darkness would last longer the farther I got from the pole.

At dusk I stopped and set up a makeshift camp beside the rover. There were still too many chasms in this area to safely travel at night.

Lying there in the sub-zero Martian night, I was suddenly gripped by a sense of loneliness. I had always been a loner and had, on occasion, spent weeks in the wilderness completely alone. My job had never been conducive to a social life. But that had never bothered me for a moment.

Now suddenly, I wondered if I was the last human alive. If it was just me... and the stars.

A few hours later, dawn began to turn the sky from deep indigo to a pink glow. I wandered over to a rocky outcrop to see if I could see some of the path ahead.

The valley was still obscured by shadows. As the weak orange orb of the sun climbed the sky, the shadows began to release their secrets. It appeared that there was a fairly level valley just to my west. This should allow a bit faster pace.

I went back to my makeshift camp, and gathered up my few posessions and set off again in the rover.

This became the routine as I slowly made my way across the face of Mars. Days came and went. It took almost two weeks to make the journey. I couldn't afford to damage the rover, so speeds were modest at best.

I occasionally tried the hand-held radio, but never heard a whisper.

I was driving through what would be considered a scenic wonderland, but somehow it still seemed hollow under the weight of the last few days.

Then, finally, the first leg of my journey came to an end.

A silvery glint in the distance told me I had located the miner. I pushed the Rover as hard as it would go as if I were afraid the gleaming machine in the distance would disappear.

As I drew closer, I could see it busily moving along sampling the soil every few meters. The miners all carried a transport pod to carry promising samples back to Earth. This was going to be my ticket off this rock.

I pulled up a few meters from the lumbering machine and stopped. I quickly located the access panel and checked the status of the transport pod. It was still fully fueled, and at about thirty percent ore capacity.

I was lucky. This one had been in a mineralogically poor area of the planet. These things were programmed to return when the load was full.

I shut down the unit and opened the airlock. A few moments later, I was breathing the first oxygen I had in weeks. Nanos or not it certainly felt comforting.

I brought the environmental services online. The temperature began to climb and I was more than happy to get out of that enviro suit.

These mining units had been built from modified military technology. Very few things in space tech weren't. These had been troop transports. They were ideally suited for the mining work. Large cargo capacity, autonomous, and easy to fit with the necessary mining equipment.

Just replace a cannon with a digger here and there, add some test equipment, change the program, and you were in business.

I went to the cockpit and began the cargo jettison sequence. I wouldn't need any ore, but I would need every last drop of fuel to get me back to Earth with the current planetary alignment.

A few moments later, I had nothing but a hold full of Martian air. A few more moments passed and it didn't even have that, as the pod climbed out of Mars' thin atmosphere and turned toward the now yellow sun.

V

Back in Space

As I began to pull away from Mars, the radio remained silent. It was as if all of humanity had disappeared.

I scanned for any nearby ship's beacon. A string of characters flashed. I ran the code through my battle computer. It was the Glasgow, a light freighter.

From her heading, she must have been coming from the Jovian system. The strong magnetosphere of Jupiter may have hidden her from the aliens, assuming they would be bothered with an unarmed ship that small.

I opened a short-range channel, "Ahoy freighter Glasgow. Are you receiving me?"

"This is Captain Cole of the Glasgow. Are you survivors from Mars?" came the reply.

"Yes Sir. Except... survivor, singular. I have heard no signals from anyone else on the surface. How many do you have?"

"There's only three of us. Me, my engineer, and my communications officer. We were on approach to Ganymede. Lucky for us, Ganymede was on the far side of Jupiter. We detected the energy discharge before we were close enough to be seen. They destroyed it. Half of Ganymede was blown away! We have been afraid to contact Earth, in case the aliens are still on the hunt. You are the first vessel we have seen since we left Jovian orbit. Who are you?"

"Colonel MacKesson, Special Services. I would like to come aboard. My ship doesn't have many amenities left."

There was a definite tone of relief in Captain Cole's voice, "Yes Sir! Glad to have you! We didn't know what we were going to do other than try to get home."

"I will be alongside in ten minutes," I said.

A few minutes later the Glasgow's airlock swung open and the gray, but alert, form of Captain Cole offered a handshake. "Welcome aboard, Colonel. Looks like a real mess we've got ourselves."

"You couldn't be more right Captain," I said as I grasped his hand. "What have you heard? Is Earth under attack?"

"Let's go to the bridge. I'll give you everything we know. There's no good news, I'm afraid," Cole said with a frown.

A short walk later, we stepped onto the bridge, and two blue uniformed people turned and looked at us expectantly.

Captain Cole gestured to the young lady, "This is Rachel Yin, my communications officer and navigator. And this is George Olafson, my engineer. Rachel, fill Colonel MacKesson in on everything you have learned."

"Aye Cap. I detected a gamma ray burst so powerful that it lit up all of Jupiter's moons on the scope. The computer triangulated it to Callisto.

"We had heard the rumors about problems with the Izars so we held position at the planet's periphery. That gave us a chance to take a peek without being too obvious.

"We got there in time to see an asteroid field with a large ship moving away from it towards Ganymede. We followed it keeping in the crescent of Jupiter.

"Fighters from the base on Ganymede flew out to meet it, but they were completely outmatched. They were vaporized in seconds. The alien ship moved near Ganymede and what looked like a huge static spark jumped to the moon... and it just exploded. The shock wave would have destroyed us had we been any closer.

"We have level six sensor recordings of the whole thing. Jupiter now has rings. There is no way anyone survived," she concluded.

"Level six recordings? On a freighter?" I queried.

"We aren't a freighter anymore. The Glasgow's been refitted for a long range survey mission." the Captain explained.

I arched an eyebrow. "A long range survey, with just you three?"

"No! No Colonel... We were delivering it to the science team on Callisto. They had been training there for over a year for a deep space mining survey," he said.

"Deep space? So she has a gravity drive?"

"I assume so. We are locked out of all but basic navigation. Security protocols. We were only expecting to fly her from Shipworks Luna to Callisto, and take the next shuttle back," Cole answered with a helpless look.

I knew the Company wouldn't be taking this level of precaution with a survey ship. She had to be something special. I would have to do some snooping around. Captain Cole didn't seem like he had much fight in him, so he shouldn't be a problem.

Ms. Yin turned suddenly, "Sirs! I have made contact with Terra! Old fashioned shortwave amplitude modulated voice!"

"On speakers!" I snapped. "Sorry Captain…"

The Captain shook his head, "It's OK Colonel. This is way above my pay grade!"

A high-pitched whine filled the room. In the distance, you could hear a voice. Too faint to be understood. The pitch of the whine dipped and rose as Rachael Yin tried to lock in on the weak signal. The noise faded and you could hear a garbled sound rumble from the speaker.

Yin looked puzzled as she looked at her display. "I have the signal, but something is distorting it."

A history book I had read as a kid flashed through my memory.

"Ham!" I exclaimed.

"Beg Pardon Colonel?" Yin said with a confused look.

I smiled, "Old style ham radio. It was used in the late 20th and early 21st centuries for hobby and emergency communications. Isolate the upper half of the wave."

The noise went silent.

"Reverse that. Isolate the lower," I ordered.

Suddenly a voice echoed across the bridge of the Glasgow.

"...ease anyone! If anyone can hear me please respond! About one hundred and fifty of us have taken refuge in Carlsbad Caverns in the Latin Union. We need help. We need food and medical supplies. Hello?"

I turned to Cole, "Supplies?"

He shook his head. "Not to my knowledge. But I have no idea what's in ninety percent of the ship."

I nodded. The Company frequently slipped high value assets through normal channels. High security only paints a target on said asset.

"Can you transmit on AM as well?" I asked Yin.

"No, Sir" she said, "Nothing which can modulate radio."

There had to be something on this ship that could be rigged to emit a brief message.

"Captain, make a cautious approach to Earth until we know what we're dealing with. We couldn't fight off a determined shuttlecraft in our current state. Plot a synchronous solar orbit and come in from sun-side. We will have a great view and the glare might give us some cover. I'm going to see what this ship really is." I said before I turned to the hatch.

"But we can't open..." Cole started.

"Trust me!" I said over my shoulder as the hatch closed behind me.

If the destination of this ship was Callisto, it meant two things. One, it damn sure wasn't a survey training mission. Callisto has been a secret military research base for some time. Two, this ship damn sure wasn't just a survey ship being sent to this base with a blind crew. Finally, I might have something to work with. I went to a computer terminal outside a large sealed hatch. I logged into it with my personal interface.

"Aha!" I thought aloud, "Standard military level one access."

I sent my identification algorithm with the emergency battlefield command string attached.

A soothing voice said, "Personal Interface authenticity confirmed. MacKesson, Robert. Colonel Special Services. Please touch the blue outlined surface for bio-function and DNA verification."

I pressed my thumb onto the small blue sensor and the panel came to life with data from hundreds of systems in every part of the ship.

"Transfer level one access to my battle computer, effective immediately." I said to the voice.

A second later, the display on the panel appeared hovering in front of me. I turned toward the closed hatch. As I approached, the locking mechanism clicked as it disengaged. As I walked, I tapped feverishly on my wrist link pulling up inventories and equipment lists. Nothing that would transmit that far on the old frequency.

I activated internal coms. "Officer Yin, report to the location highlighted on your console immediately."

An acknowledgment light blinked. I hurried on to the radar room. As I awaited Yin to arrive, I noticed the normal external communication status as active. I opened the channel to see what was going on.

"… just barely got away with our lives. The signal is a trap! It's madness. They waited until we were on close approach to land and then opened fire. The Sprite was in front of us and caught most of the fire. She crashed, ablaze. Warn everyone you see not to respond!" a strange, disheveled man said.

I cut into the channel. "Who? Who attacked you?"

Suddenly the man looked even more rattled, if possible, "Sir? People sir! The ones transmitting the distress call! They were waiting for us with projectile explosives!"

I couldn't see a rank insignia on him. "What's your name and rank?"

"Rank? We're not military… we're contractors. We were doing some ore sampling in the asteroid belt when all hell broke loose!"

"OK, calm down. What's your name, son?" I asked trying to keep him from panicking.

"Higgs."

"OK Higgs, I'm Colonel MacKesson. Have you contacted anyone else?"

"We picked up two people in a life pod in low Earth orbit. Their ship was destroyed, by fire from Earth. They say that the surface was almost wiped out. Nearly every city was hit with some sort of fusion weapon," he said.

"Can you put one of them on?"

Shortly, a smeared face appeared. Hidden under dirt and terror was a young woman. I wondered to myself if she would be able to talk coherently.

Before I could begin, she started on her own. "We were on Earth when the alien ships arrived," she said with a shake of her head and a sudden look of anger.

"Alerts went out. They said Jupiter, Saturn, and Mars had all been attacked and the aliens were coming here. Every government sent every ship they had. The sky was on fire. No one on earth could miss it. As the fight drew nearer, we began to see that the debris raining down wasn't from an alien force; it was our ships being destroyed one by one by a single, massive ship.

"It was almost crystalline in shape. It was destroying earth forces with no more regard than we would swat a bug.

"They said it went into a low polar orbit. It obliterated every city and town they passed over.

"A few of us were stationed in the remote Sierra Nevada's at an old missile silo that was converted into a relay station. We had an old low orbit shuttle in one of the bays... it hadn't been used in years. It had been safe from the electromagnetic pulse.

"We worked on it for days until we had engines and life support. When we took off we quickly came under fire. They seemed to be shooting at anything in the air. We took several hits but thought we had made it until one of the engines went critical. Six made it into life-pods before the shuttle exploded. We were the only ones to make it to low orbit. The other two life-pods burned up in the atmosphere. We would have burned up by now too if the Helix hadn't picked us up..." her voice broke as emotion flooded her face. She withdrew from the screen.

Higgs reappeared. "We're heading to Luna Base to try to find refuge."

"Is there any indication who fired on you?" I questioned.

"No. But after the attack, everyone was expecting an invasion. All of the resistance teams were told to consider all aircraft hostile.

"OK. Standby where you are and we will rendezvous and take you aboard." I told him.

"Look, Colonel," he said with anger creeping into his voice, "the earth governments are gone, the company is gone. We don't take orders from anyone anymore. We're going to the moon. You would be smart to join us."

I had to admit, at least to myself, that he had a point. Rachael Yin had ran in during all this, and had occupied herself with one of the terminals in the room, as I was already dealing with the event she came to tell me about.

"Colonel, there's a missile coming up from the planet," she yelled across the room, "it is moving to intercept the Helix. Sir! The Helix has no chance against that missile."

"Follow me!" I told Yin and we sprinted down the corridor. My virtual display guided me to the ships real bridge. The door opened and a sea of lights awakened around the entire bridge.   A holographic display emerged from a pedestal in the center.   An image of Earth appeared with a red target moving up from the surface toward a green target.   The red meaning the armed missile, the green was the defenseless Helix.

"Call the others down here.   It's time to show this bird's true colors." I said as I looked up at the insignia on the wall.   **IPS X1 Phantom.**

VI

On Board the Phantom

The Captain was happy to assume the role of Executive Officer on the Phantom. He knew little about her, but he knew the people, and how to run a ship.

I looked around from the center seat, "Mister Yin, how long till bogey makes contact?"

"Three minutes, twelve seconds," she said. "Receiving urgent messages from the Helix."

I glanced toward her and said, "Understood. Advise Helix that we will not allow her to come to harm, and to continue on course."

Cole stepped over to me and asked, "What's the plan Colonel?"

"Mister Cole, let me introduce you to the IPS Phantom, stealth cruiser," I said.

I activated the pilot's controls on the Captain's chair, and a panel emerged and swung in front of me.

A gesture activated the camouflage jettison, and a row of dark screens around the perimeter of the room began to show an image as the cargo containers that had encased the ship drifted away.

Now the external cameras showed us all what we were actually in. The Phantom was a sleek craft resembling an eagle with sweptback wings. A pair of nasty looking plasma cannons hung under each wing. One hell of a 'survey' ship.

A gesture brought up the guidance system, and seconds later the gravity drive hurled us the three hundred million kilometers to Earth's orbit in under a minute.

I pulled up the targeting scanners and locked onto the missile's image.

Ms. Yin sang out, "Missile changing course, Sir! We're the new target."

Our targeting scanner had, expectedly, provoked a priority target change for the missile.

The image of the missile on the screen was framed in red as the computer indicated a target lock. I pressed my thumb to a box on the Captain's display. The box turned green and the firing button glowed ready. As I touched the bright red button, the plasma cannons sprayed a searing blue-white beam at the missile, vaporizing it in a silent flash.

"Ms. Yin, Helix on speakers please," I said.

She nodded ready.

"That was probably a remaining missile that was triggered by the fires. You were just the nearest target it could sense, I don't think you are under attack," I reassured him.

"I hope you're right. It wouldn't take much of an attack to wipe out whatever few survivors who are lucky enough to make it to Luna Base," returned Higgs' nervous voice.

"I think the important thing now is to find out the condition of Luna Base. We may be headed for a non-existent refuge," I thought aloud. "We will go on ahead and see what it looks like, Mr. Higgs."

"Thanks Colonel. Helix out" and the channel fell silent.

The stars turned bluish as the gravity drive distorted space. In little more than a second, we were in lunar orbit. As the ground passed swiftly by below us we saw a burned wreckage field come into view. It extended over the horizon. "Mister Cole, what do you make of this?" I asked.

"Colonel, according to these readings, this is what's left of Shipworks Luna," he replied with a quiver in his voice, "There were ten thousand souls aboard that station…"

In a few moments, the outline of Luna Base came into view. A number of shapes around the base resolved into ships as we neared.

"Scans indicate no damage to the base. They still have power and pressure," Yin said. "There are twenty-three small ships there."

"It would appear they are OK. Still no comms with them?" I asked.

"Not a peep, sir" she replied, "Maybe they are afraid of attracting attention?"

"Possible... signal the Helix to proceed. We're going in. Mr. Cole, see if you can find us a place to park," I said.

VII

Luna Base

There was a grind and hiss as the inner airlock door swung open to reveal three assault rifles pointed at us.

"Easy Guys! I'm Colonel MacKesson, Special Services," I said in a measured tone.

"Lower your weapons! They're human!" a young voice said from farther up the corridor. "Lieutenant Greyson, sir. Sorry for the frosty welcome. We didn't recognize the ship, and couldn't take the risk, Colonel. We haven't got the eternal comms working yet."

"You acted properly, Lieutenant. Who is in command?" I queried.

"I am, sir. I mean I was, and you are now sir!"

"At ease there. I think we can forgo the formalities in this situation. Just call me Mac," I said. This kid couldn't be more than nineteen, fresh out of Officer Candidate School, no doubt.

Another young man came running up looking anxious, "Lt. Greyson! We have another inbound ship! Survey class."

I spoke up, "That will be the Helix. She's Okay."

"Very good sir!" he sputtered and disappeared down the corridor.

"Mr. Greyson, I need a full debriefing on everything that has happened to you since the attack," I said as we walked into the command center. "What is your first name, son?" I asked.

"Wesley, sir."

"Do you go by Wes? And it's Mac."

"Yes sir... Mac."

I nodded, "Okay Wes, catch me up."

He took a deep breath. "I was the supply officer on the Sargasso. We were a light cruiser refitted into a glorified taxi for dignitaries, but Admiral Bennett ordered every vessel to stand and defend Earth.

"We had minimal weaponry. We flew diplomatic missions. Many cultures won't give an armed foreign vessel docking permission.

I was on the bridge when the Captain told the Admiral. Do you know what he said? Do you know what he said? He said we might draw fire away from a useful ship!

When the alien ship arrived it became obvious that Earth's forces were ridiculously out-matched."

I cut in, "Tell me about the ship, its fighters…"

Wes jerked his head as if trying to avoid looking at an image in his mind.

"There were no fighters. Just one massive ship. Our fleet had no chance. They were pouring everything they had at that ship, but nothing penetrated to the hull. They had an energy shield that even our nukes couldn't crack. One shot. That's what it took to destroy the Valiant. Our last heavy cruiser they said.

"The Sargasso was hit by debris from a nearby exploding battleship. It took out our engines when it embedded itself three decks deep in our underbelly. Captain Mitchell gave the order to abandon ship, but the bridge crew either didn't make it to the escape pods or they were destroyed in the debris field. Gone. They're all dead." Wes said with some disbelief at his own words.

He continued, "We arrived here and one by one the other ships arrived. Mostly courier ships, commercial vessels and dedicated runs that were lucky enough to be in space when it occurred. We were the only survivors of the battle to make it back."

I could see him slipping away, "Wes. Pull it together. First order of business: survival. Have you gotten inventories and status reports from base crew?"

Another haunted look crossed his face, "Base crew? There were no survivors here."

I stiffened. "No survivors?"

"No. We moved the bodies to external storage," he said.

"There didn't appear to be any damage to the base when we flew over. What killed them?" I asked urgently. I hoped I was wrong in what I was thinking.

"Loss of air. The place was a total vacuum. When no one responded to open the gantry, we landed and came in through the airlock. It was kind of odd. The pressure came back up quickly when we brought power back online. The only thing that is still down is the gantry door. We haven't figured it out yet," Wes explained.

I caught my breath. "It's a trap. This whole place."

"How... how do you know?" he asked glancing nervously around.

"The Izars have destroyed every other human outpost they have come across, and they leave Shipworks Luna spread across the Sea of Tranquility, but they leave one which would be an obvious rally point for survivors."

"But why kill the crew first? Surely they would have guided more survivors here," Wes offered.

"They needed to plant a booby trap. Get your best people together. We have to find our surprise and quick. We may not have much time," I said.

"Shouldn't we evacuate?" Wes asked.

George Olafson spoke up, "That sounds like a plan to me, Mac!"

"To where? Those aren't deep space ships out there, and none of them are shielded for re-entry. They were built in space for use in space. I doubt most of them have rations for even a week. This base has everything we need. It is designed to be self-sustaining. We need to keep it if we have any hope of survival in the short term. If we're careful, we can live in here quite a while," I explained.

George looked a bit pale at this revelation. Cole nodded and Yin held the same steely look of determination that she had when I first met her.

Before I could continue, Wes returned with about a dozen even younger men and women.

"Mac, sir. This is the rest of my crew. They're good people," he said breathlessly.

"No time for introductions. Where can we have a little privacy?" I asked.

"This way," Wes said as he led us into what appeared to be the base commander's office.

Before the echo of the hatch closing died, I was telling them my suspicions.

"Now what I need from you all is to search this base from top to bottom. Concentrate on critical areas and on areas where you are most familiar with the systems and equipment. Look for anything odd which might be a bomb, or something that just doesn't look right. Anything that looks as if it doesn't belong is to be reported at once," I said gazing from frightened face to frightened face.

I turned to the Phantom crew, "George, you're our engineer. Get down to the reactor and go over it with a microscope. If we lose that, it's game over. Mr. Cole, I want you in environmental. Rachael, coordinate. Keep each team in radio contact. Don't waste time, and keep this top secret. We will have a panic to deal with if this gets out. Everyone in a different direction, MOVE!" I barked.

I turned to Rachael and gave her my battle computer frequency. "I'm going to see what I can get out of the computer logs. If you turn up anything, let me know ASAP."

She nodded, "Wilco. One question though... why are you so certain this place is rigged?"

"It's the only explanation that fits all the facts. First, when you wipe out a planet, the people off-world will be back, and will be looking for safe harbor" I explained.

"The Luna Base?"

"Exactly. Why chase down dozens to hundreds of small ships, when you can wait for them to set up home in your trap? And first step to do such a thing would be-"

Rachael cut me off, "Dispose of the base inhabitants!"

"Exactly. Couple that with the gantry door being the only thing damaged, forcing everyone to have to use an airlock to get to their ships in an emergency," I said.

"But what," she queried, "would be the trigger? A timer? Remote?"

I paused, "Not if I were doing it. How many airlocks does this base have?"

Rachael consulted her portable display, "The one we came in, and one other. Oh, and one for the rover."

"Ask Wes if anyone has taken the rover out since they arrived. I doubt it, but ask to be sure," I told her.

A second later, she replied in the negative. Her eyes told me she had reached the same conclusion. In a base wide emergency, everyone was trained go to the biggest airlock. We dashed down the corridor in the direction of the rover bay.

VIII

A Big Problem

We reached the rover bay quickly in the Moon's weak gravity. When you were in a hurry, you immediately realized why the base was built with two-meter high corridors. When you tried to run, you bounded more than ran. The rover bay was dark. Rachael activated the lights and we walked up to the airlock. Nothing seemed amiss. We spent several minutes scrutinizing every piece of hardware but found nothing.

Rachael turned to me and asked, "Do you think we could be wrong?"

I shook my head in frustration. I was right. I knew it in my gut. "Maybe, but I don't think so."

I walked over to the observation window and peered inside at the rover. Suddenly it hit me. I turned to the console and began sifting through the screens.

"What are you doing?" she asked.

I smiled. "We're not beat yet. I have an idea. Any word from the search teams?"

"Nothing useful" she answered glancing at her display.

"I'm activating the rover's remote link. That science pack is going to save our collective asses," I muttered as much to myself as Rachael.

A large display lit up with an image of the outer lock hatch.

"We're in!" I exclaimed as I rotated the camera to look at the backside of our hatch.

Rachael's hand flew up and pointed at the screen. "There!"

"I see it," I said as I zoomed the camera in on a black box attached to the inner face of the hatch near the hatch wheel. Some strange characters blinked silently. I could see a thin, transparent probe protruding through the wheel. I activated record and set the robotic camera to image, in maximum resolution, every inch of the inside of the door.

"Rachael, post a guard outside this room. No one enters. Alert the entire base that the emergency evac system is being serviced, and to ignore any alarms," I ordered. "Let's get back to control and analyze this footage."

Rachael stopped, hand at her ear, "Sir! Mister. Cole has found something!"

"He's in the environmental plant," I said as I pulled up the base map, "let's go!"

A few minutes later, we were standing in front of an access panel to a huge air pipe.

Cole was pale and rather disheveled. "Mac, it's bad! There are charges on the inside of the return pipe, about halfway to the enviro plant. That's a ten-foot return duct. If they go, it will pump this place to a vacuum in a minute. I didn't touch anything. I'm guessing you're going in?"

"Definitely. Get me a tool pack and a hand scanner," I said.

Rachael emerged from a locker with a small bag and tossed it to me. "If you don't need me, I shall call off the search and get to analyzing the video of the airlock," she said.

"No, continue the search. These are some clever bastards," I said.

I turned to the access panel. "Floodlight?" I asked, and Cole proffered one. "Open it up!"

"You might want full magnet gear in there or you could end up in a filter," Cole suggested, gesturing to a pair of magnetic coveralls for hull access in space, but these had obviously been modified for indoor use.

"Good idea," I said as I went to pull them on.

Cole popped the single remaining catch and the small door flew open with a bang as a deafening blast of air pushed me back a step.

I pushed my way forward against the rush of air to the small door and poked my head through. The wind was deafening and felt as if it were trying to pull my hair out. I slapped the energize button for the mag coveralls and felt my hand clamp to the metal. A short jump and I was inside the huge duct.

I seated a floodlight firmly on the curved wall and directed its beam down the tunnel. At least in this wind the chances of a booby-trapped explosive were slim.

They were located where no one would find them without a deliberate search. I could see three shapes equidistantly spaced on the steel walls of the duct about ten meters in front of me.

I staggered awkwardly forward in the mag suit. In the low gravity, I would have had no chance of clinging onto the smooth inside of the pipe without it.

I stopped a few feet from the devices and set up two more floodlights. There was a small light blinking in sync with the other devices. There were no other outside features on the small black boxes.

I was still there, so obviously there were no proximity sensors. Hopefully the scanner wouldn't trigger anything.

I passed the scan tool's emitter over the lower box and watched images of its components coalesce into recognizable shapes. Elemental symbols scrolled down the side of the display indicating the composition of the bit under the cross hairs. Some things I recognized, but the principal component was a type of interlaced polymer that I had never seen before. It was incredibly dense. The molecules of the polymer were intertwined with the molecules of the pipe itself.

This was beyond any Earth technology I had ever seen. It was as if the solid block molecularly welded the device to the pipe.

I pulled a small bladed tool from the bag and tried to scrape off a sample of the material, but my blade wouldn't make a mark.

I decided to retreat to the control room to analyze these readings and see how Rachael was getting on.

About halfway there, my battle computer flashed a message from control. Greyson had gone on to find another device connected to the heating system. Scans were coming into control now.

I came into a flurry of activity in the control room. News had leaked out, but rather than panic, it seemed to instill a determination in the survivors. A goal. A chance to beat some small aspect of the Izar's plan.

"We have to do something, and soon. This other device that's connected to our heating system," Rachael began, "appears to trigger when our enviro system switches from cool to heat with the sunset. The only good news is that sunset isn't for another three Terran days. That gives us time to disarm these things. They didn't understand our system very well. I think it would have triggered the system's warnings."

I shook my head. "Disarming isn't an option on the explosives. They are molecularly bonded with some unknown ultra-dense material. I couldn't mark it, and the use of power tools on bombs was frowned upon in mercenary school," I said wryly.

"You haven't looked at the analysis of your scans yet," she said. "It gets better. That ultra-dense material IS the explosive."

I rubbed my eyes and said, "Great. We have bombs we can't even understand, much less disarm, that are going to trigger when our heating system kicks on to keep us from freezing to death. Wes, was the heating system off when you arrived?"

He nodded, "All enviro was offline."

"So let's go over what we know. This base was rigged to lie in wait for the first people to come inside and turn environmental back on. People come and do. They are happy. They signal others to come. Sunset comes and boom? Why the airlock device? What if they didn't make a mistake on the heating system device? What if it were to trigger the evac alarm?" I thought aloud.

Rachael spoke up, "If anyone spins the wheel to open that hatch it will trigger the explosive. That is clear from the scans."

I nodded, "Okay, that sends the crew all running to the airlock which will fit the most people to meet an explosion; while simultaneously the air duct is blown, suffocating any stragglers."

Wesley stepped forward. "What if we just turn the environmental systems back off and suit up for the night?" he asked.

Rachael smiled, "Your suit can't handle that long! We won't see sunlight again for two weeks!"

He gave her a sheepish look after his rookie mistake, "Sorry. I should have remembered that!"

"Get George Olafson up here," I said.

The chatter continued while I waited for George, with people tossing ideas back and forth. None of them seemed to have the potential to address the whole problem.

"You sent for me, Mac?" George asked.

"Yes. Do you think you could put together a decent engineering team out of this lot?" I inquired, "They will need to work outside and work fast."

George looked away thoughtfully. "What's the job?"

"Heating duct repair. They will need to weld, cut... you know, the usual. It really depends on how bad it is. Take a look at these images," I told him.

He nodded, "I think I can do you one better, sir," he tapped away on a computer terminal. "There's some extra pipe that came in for a construction job which never materialized. We could have one of those standing by to do a fast swap of the whole section!"

I couldn't hide the grin, "Feel free to show me up anytime you like, George!" In a more serious tone I added, "It's about time something broke in our favor."

He gave me a knowing look. "I'll get on with preparations in that case."

"How long will you need?"

"A day and a half at least. In addition to getting the part and equipment in place, I have to make sure that I have qualified welders, and if not I have to qualify some pretty damned fast. A bad weld and we're just as dead."

"Good plan. Just be sure to stage out of the range of the blast."

"Aye, aye," George shouted over his shoulder as he departed.

Rachael walked up and said, "Okay. It looks like we might pull this off. How much damage to you estimate when the airlock blows?"

"We will mount an actuator on the hatch wheel to trigger the bomb. Next, open the outer door, to give the blast another way to go. Then pull everyone out of that section and purge the atmosphere," I paused and rubbed my eyes, "that should limit the damage.

"However, since we are dealing with an unknown explosive, all of this may be for nothing. That could be enough to level half the moon for all we know."

"Do you think that's likely?" she questioned.

I shook my head, "The physical evidence doesn't support that hypothesis. Why have a charge on the airlock, plus three in the duct, if a single charge on the outside would destroy the place."

"You have a tendency to make people feel everything's going to be okay," she said with a smile. "When's the last time you've slept?"

"I can't remember," I admitted.

"Go to the CO's quarters, have a shower, and get some sleep. George is in his element with this, and Wes and I can take care of the rest for the moment. I'm sure the late CO wouldn't mind in these circumstances," Rachael said. "Besides, I have a feeling we're going to need you at your best when the booms go off!"

I chuckled to myself, "I yield to the logic of your argument!" I hadn't realized how tired I was until the crisis had reached a plateau. "Wake me if anything unanticipated happens," I said as I left the room to the echo of several 'good nights'.

IX

Explosions are Silent in Space

The next day passed in a blur. After grabbing a few hours' sleep, I sent Rachael and Wes to do the same.

George was like a starving bulldog with a bone on this project, refusing to stop for anything. He had handpicked his team of eight welders and four laser cutters. He had explained to me that it was too dangerous for anyone to be inside the pipe while it was being cut, but they could weld inside and out simultaneously.

It seemed we were as ready as we had any hope of being.

I stood up and cleared my throat. The control room fell silent. "Open all internal channels please," a nod from a young man sitting at communications indicated the ready.

"Ladies and gentlemen, we have faced the most devastating enemy in the history of mankind. We few have not fallen to the malevolent wishes of our enemy, and we aren't going to today! All non-essential personnel evacuate immediately to the Phantom. Remaining personnel should already be in space suits and moving to sections D and E. Prepare for depressurization in ten minutes. Everyone must focus on what you, specifically, have to do. If everybody does this, everybody lives. MacKesson out."

George and his crew were standing by in the bottom of a small, nearby crater. It was just deep enough to keep them out of any blast wave. The team which was assigned to the inside welding detail sheltered in the farthest sections from the duct. I was going with the team assigned to repair the airlock. I had split them in two with one standing by in section E and the other sheltering outside with me. We were the closest to the explosions, but had good cover behind a large boulder.

When I arrived to meet the airlock team, they were suited and preparing to exit the airlock.

They exited in pairs as I quickly donned my suit, and exited with their fifth man.

I quickly did a visual scan of the area as the team took cover. "Rachael?" I asked into the communicator.

"Right here, Colonel. Airlock actuator online and showing green. George signals that they are in position," she said.

"Good. Mr. Cole?"

"Everyone secure aboard the Phantom," Cole's voice boomed over the Phantom's powerful transmitters.

"Proceed Ms. Yin," I said evenly.

Everyone's head turned toward me as all communication channels went live.

"All personnel brace for impact," Rachael's voice said, "Detonation in three… two…"

There was a flash just visible in the open airlock, and a brighter flash from the pipe that was immediately obscured by dust and debris thrown outward from the explosion point.

I quickly hit all call on my transmitter. "HOLD! Everyone hold where they are for one minute," and I switched to the control frequency. "Rachael, can you confirm airlock detonation?"

"Standby," came the reply. "Camera's coming online now... yes. There is a hole in the door. There doesn't seem to be much more damage."

"Affirmative," I said as I switched back to all call. "Go. All teams proceed as assigned."

By the time I had closed the channel I could see a line of people filing out of the crater and we had covered half the distance to our target. I wasn't staying with the repair detail; I just wanted to see firsthand what the alien explosive had done.

The damage to the airlock was minimal. That I accredited to the lack of air in the base. An explosive's destructive power comes from the pressure wave in the air. With no air, the pressure wave dissipates very rapidly. I picked up a fragment of twisted metal for analysis and headed back out to George's team.

I switched to the pipe team's channel and was greeted by the Norwegian's deep voice directing one person after another. A three-meter section of pipe in a sort of cradle/trailer was being pulled into position.

George seemed to be conducting a symphony of people and machines. "… Rotate the wheels ninety degrees. Okay, now bring her forward into place. A little more… perfect!" Now taker her up!"

The pipe slowly began to rise as the concealed scissor lift struggled to raise the load, even in lunar gravity.

"Watch out! Stop!" George shouted.

I turned back in time to see the huge pipe begin to lean. It was impossible for the men on the end of the ropes to slow its great bulk. The huge pipe rolled over as the ground under one of the wheels gave way.

"Get out of there! Drop those ropes and jump!" George bellowed as he tore his way toward the unfolding scene.

I took off as fast as I could, knowing there was nothing I could do. The comms system was an incoherent babble. There wasn't time to quiet everyone, so I tapped George on the shoulder and signaled him to change channels.

"Mac, I've got two men trapped under there!" he said with desperation in his voice.

"What do we have that can lift this thing?" I asked, "This lift is shot."

George shook his head, "Nothing. Nothing, Mac. This was the only one." He turned and joined the men trying to dig out the victims.

I briefed Rachael on what was happening.

"What about the Phantom?" she asked, "That piece of steel would weigh nothing to her!"

"But the thrusters would incinerate anyone below. We have to lift it into position and hold it for the welders, and we're running out of time! I need ideas!" I snapped into the microphone.

George half-walked half stumbled over to me. "It's too late. They're dead..."

I took him roughly by the arm, "Engineer! You have a job to do or we ALL die! Understood?"

His eyes hardened, "Aye, sir!" and he turned back to his crew and began barking orders, then turned back to me and said, "Mac, I think we can use the Phantom. Move her over here near the pipe and use her grapple to pull the pipe back in line. We will build a skid-ramp out of steel to guide it high enough."

I thought about that and glanced at the sun nearing the horizon. "Do we have time for that? We will have to move the pipe the other way a good bit to make room for your ramp to align properly."

"No sir. We can do it with a much shorter ramp. If we get it high enough we can pass a beam through it from the other pipe, and then jack it up from the inside into perfect alignment for the welders," he explained.

I was impressed. "Sounds good! I will get the Phantom into position," I said as I switched channels to coordinate with Rachael.

Cole had moved the Phantom into position, and her grapple easily pulled the huge pipe up the ramp. A few moments later the section of pipe began to rise to meet its final position between the two carefully cut ends of our vital air supply. Cole returned the Phantom to her position nearer the airlock as figures scurried over the pipe with welding lasers shining. It was only an hour after dark when re-pressurization began.

X

Recon

After a few days, reasonable calm had again permeated the base, and I summoned the Glasgow crew to meet in my quarters to discuss our next mission.

The banging on my compartment hatch jarred me from thought. "Enter," I said loudly.

The wheel spun and the hatch swung open revealing Rachael Yin, Mr. Cole, and George Olafson.

"Come in and have a seat," I said, gesturing to a small round table standing in a pool of light supporting a pot of coffee and a stack of cups.

We all sat, and Cole was the first to break the ice. "What new slice of alien hell do you have for us today, Mac?"

I gave him a dry smile. "Just easy stuff this time. A little PR work! I have spoken to a few of you about this, but now we need to convince our populace to make some hard choices. This base was originally designed to be self-sustaining for a crew of twenty-five. Before we arrived, it had a crew of seventy-five. It could not survive without help from Earth. We don't have the knowledge, manpower, or materials. Food will run out in about two more months. There is zero probability of getting a hydroponic system producing sufficient food to feed everyone even if we had the parts to build one or the seeds to plant. As I see it, there is only one option. Everyone must return to Earth, so we are going on a reconnaissance mission to aid that end.

Rachael spoke up first, "What do you have in mind?"

I pulled up a brightly colored holographic display of Earth. "The red areas are dead zones. Intensely radioactive. Yellow, physical exposure is okay, but avoid inhaling dust and don't eat or drink anything. The green areas are still contaminated, but not lethally. Unfortunately, there's nowhere

113

untouched. We know what kind of reception the Helix received, but we don't know if everyone feels the same about visitors from above. Communications are somewhere between crippled and non-existent on the surface now. There could be short range comms that we can't detect, but so far nothing since the last short wave message was intercepted a couple of weeks ago. What we are going to do is land, and try to make contact," I said.

Rachael Yin leaned forward with a hard expression, "What if we come under attack? Can we defend ourselves?"

I nodded, "We will all be armed, but there won't be any need to go above the stun level. We're there to make friends. There are probably no energy weapons still functional after the electromagnetic pulses from the detonations, so risk is minimal. The main danger will be old style projectile weapons, in which case wide beam stun will be more effective than kill at halting an attacker."

I glanced around the table at everyone's faces. I felt I could depend on them.

"Okay," I said, "getting to specifics. Most of the green areas are in extreme latitudes. We know many of these places had small to medium populations, but some have never been inhabited. We are going to overfly as many as we can while scanning for human life signs. If there is a small native village they will be less likely to be hostile than you might find in the remains of a large city. That will be out contact target."

"Will they be likely to have any useful knowledge if they are isolated and incommunicado?" Commander Cole inquired.

"No," I answered, "but this is more to see how receptive they are to outsiders."

"Ah, I understand," he said

I continued, "I have no doubt there are hostiles down there just looking for someone to fight. We aren't looking for these people. We don't want them to have any idea we were there. That would only fan the flames. If we can make contact with enough friendly villages who would just take in a few people, then their chances of survival increase dramatically."

George Olafson chuckled, "Go in at maximum stealth just to stop and say 'Hello!'"

Muted laughter moved around the table.

"Yes, I think you've got a firm grasp on the situation, George!" I smiled.

I stood up and said, "If no one has any questions, we lift off in one hour."

Everyone stood and filed out of the room, and I went in search of Lieutenant Wes Greyson.

Wes was having lunch with a couple of his staff. One was an older brunette lady with a severe haircut. Wes introduced her as Emily Glass, Captain of the Radian, a light freight/courier ship under military contract. The other was a Systems Engineer by the name of Herbert "call me Herb" Pickard who was traveling aboard the Radian when the attack began. The introductions concluded, and I indicated I would like to speak to Wes alone.

"Have a seat, Colonel," Wes said as the others departed.

I smiled, "Don't mind if I do!" I said as I slid into the seat opposite. "The Glasgow crew and I are going to be gone for a few days."

A look of concern crept onto his face, "Gone, Sir?"

"Yes," I said, "a recon mission. Have you looked at our inventory? It's not a pleasant read," I said without waiting for an answer. "With the number of people we have here, it would require beyond perfect yield from the hydroponics bay just to maintain starvation level nourishment. The stores will be gone in weeks at the rate we're going through them. Short rations would only prolong the inevitable anyway."

Wes paled at this realization. "So what is the plan?"

I leaned forward. "We," I said, "are going back to Earth. I will have a lot more to tell you when we get back. I wanted to brief you as much as I could before we go, but keep this confidential. No point telling anyone anything until we know what to tell them. Plus, if this gets out on its own, you

117

will need to put the fires out. The last things we need are fights breaking out over food."

"Got it! If it goes public," Wes said, "our official position is we are aware of the problem and have a plan."

"That is a fact beyond question!" I smiled, adding in my head, "even if a plan had little chance of working, it was still a plan!"

I had stood to leave when Wes asked, "What if you… um… fail to return?"

"Then every life here will be in your hands," I told him soberly.

He nodded, and I turned for the newly repaired hangar.

We returned to Earth on conventional thrusters. It was risky using the gravity drive near massive objects. If you hit a natural gravitational wave at the wrong moment, you could be slammed into a planet like a bug on a windshield.

"Officer Yin, focus every scanner we have on the planet. We're going to orbit here for a little

118

while and take an inventory of what's still standing," I ordered as I guided the Phantom into a low polar trajectory. "This should give us details down to the local bacteria count."

"Data recorders active on all bands," Yin said.

"Give us a live map of radiation levels on the main display, please."

A moment later an outline of continents appeared on the screen. A red bar along the side of the screen indicated the pre-attack population as 5.8 billion people. As human life signs were detected, a small number at the bottom of the screen increased and changed the red bar to green. The green was almost invisible.

We watched in silence as, pass after pass, the number grew agonizingly slowly. By the time we made our final orbit, the human tally was a mere forty-one thousand, one hundred and twenty-eight people alive on the surface of the Earth.

Most in small pockets of less than fifty, but a number of islands with a thousand or more. The cities were reduced to lava fields. There was nothing left. Man had been returned to the middle ages in less than a day. Almost a millennium of development erased. A painful lesson in humility indeed.

In a matter of hours, we had completed our scans of the surface. "Prepare for re-entry. Let's take a look at some promising real estate," I said as I angled the Phantom downward toward our scorched home. A sonic boom from our re-entry echoed across an empty five-mile wide harbor where New York City used to stand. The sea had rushed into the molten crater, seemingly to erase the land itself where the great city once reached skyward. As we moved southwest crossing the Americas, we could see that firestorms had charred the entire landscape... fields, forests, nothing had escaped. I turned in a westerly heading toward Hawaii. The outline of the island chain appeared on the monitor and quickly passed beneath us, but the islands didn't. They had disappeared beneath the waves.

I heard a soft sound come from behind me on the bridge, and glanced back to see tears flowing down Rachael's cheek.

"Ms. Yin, lay in our overflight course please," I said giving her an understanding look.

She wiped at her eyes and responded, "Aye, aye, Colonel."

A few minutes later a dark shape on the horizon resolved into a chain of islands. They were littered with debris in all but the highest points from tsunamis.

I broke the silence, "Navigator, report."

Rachael spoke with renewed determination in her voice, "The volcanic chain of Tonga, sir. There were one hundred and forty-six life signs detected, all on the big island ahead. Radiation levels green."

"Have you found us a landing site?" I asked.

"Coordinates going in now," came the reply.

I turned the phantom toward a red dot that appeared highlighting a clearing near the shore.

Seconds later, we were sitting softly in the sand. I opened the main gantry and said, "Everyone wait here. No point risking more necks than necessary," automatically raising my hand to silence the protest. "I will keep the channel open on my battle computer. You will see and hear everything I do," I said to quash the dissent.

A few moments later my foot touched Earth's soil for the first time in what seemed like eons. I took a deep breath of the salty air and began to work my way past the piles of debris toward a life sign indicator flashing in front of me courtesy of my battle computer. Apparently they had seen us come in, as the life signs were coming closer, but still over a kilometer away. I climbed a hill above the tsunami line and found a trail that led to a road. I started toward the signal at a brisk jog, surprised at the lack of muscle loss for so much time in low gravity without time for exercise. Then the memory of the stinging pain of the nano injection offered an answer. They must somehow maintain muscle tone in low gravity. "That, I could get used to!" I thought.

I heard a low buzzing sound in the distance, and I could just make out a shape approaching in the distance. Slowly approaching. As it drew nearer, or rather I drew nearer to it took on the shape of a mini bike ridden by a portly, middle-aged islander.

"Hello!" he shouted as he waved furiously.

I waved back and a few seconds later, we met.

"About bloody time you lot remembered us!" he said in a heavy Australian accent. "The others will be along shortly; this wonky old thing is the only engine working on the whole island!"

I took his outstretched hand, and said "I'm afraid you have the wrong idea, we're not a rescue party."

"You're not?"

"No, closer to refugees, I'm afraid. I'm Rob MacKesson, if we can go to your village, I will catch you up on everything that has happened," I told him.

He scratched his head and asked, "Are you alone?"

"No," I answered, "there are three more waiting in the ship. May they join us there?"

"Yes, of course! My name is Bruce Tupou Jones. My great-great-great grandpa was the King of Tonga!" he said proudly as he slid his little bike around to the opposite direction. "Follow me!" he yelled as he roared off at about walking speed.

I let him get a few yards ahead and said, "It seems okay. Rendezvous with me at the village. Take a display with you so you can monitor my feed. See you there."

A short walk later, I was greeted warmly by a large group of mostly natives. They led me to a large yard behind a row of houses with dozens of assorted seats scattered about beneath the trees.

Bruce introduced me to a group of young to middle-aged people who seemed to speak for the inhabitants. As he was finishing, the Phantom's crew arrived and the introductions started again.

Once that was behind us, I briefed them on what we knew about the attack, the state of Earth, and the few survivors. They stared with incredulity at the scenes of destruction that flashed over Rachael's display.

"So we're on our own," said a man introduced as Kai. "We heard the reports of the attack coming, and many left for the mainland. Most of us couldn't afford to go. I guess that was a good thing. We saw burning debris in the sky and a little while later all of the phones and radios stopped working, then the rest of the electronics."

"Bruce was able to rig up that old bike with an old lawnmower engine, and that's the only thing that still runs on the island," someone chimed in.

Kai nodded and continued, "Then the tsunamis hit. The first one came from the west and killed hundreds near the beaches. Then more came from the south, then every other direction. We have no idea how many were swept out to sea. It was so fast we didn't have time to rescue anyone," he ended sadly.

I explained our predicament and they were receptive to the idea of more settlers, as they would need all the help they could get rebuilding their island. They were a warm and friendly people who were paying the price for an offense committed light-years away. I told them to expect the new arrivals in the next few days.

Landing after landing followed this same pattern. Stunned silence followed by the defiant human will to move forward.

After we had confirmed plenty of suitable sites, we turned and headed back to Luna Base with this new data.

On arrival, I called a meeting of the acting senior staff. It was time that we formed a plan to end the space age of man. I described our trip back to Earth to them, and guided them through the data.

"Wide swaths of radiation belt the planet," I said as images flashed across the display at the front of the room. "Radiation signatures indicated a fusion weapon. With any luck, the surface should recover in a few decades. The weapon they used doesn't appear to have spread radioactivity, rather the reaction itself irradiated the area. I'm guessing the Izars found no need to kill the patient with the disease, as this radiation will fade to safe levels in a few years. In short, Earth will recover, and pretty quickly. Mankind, however… is now an endangered species."

An older gentleman that I didn't know spoke up, "Sir, tell us. How many people were lost?"

I took a deep breath and gave them the news, "We may never know the exact number of dead. We detected a little over forty-one thousand human life signs remaining on the surface of Earth."

The room seemed to gasp as one. Murmurs went around the table as people realized that everyone they knew was probably dead. Some cried. Some sat in stony silence.

Wes spoke, "We will rebuild. It may take years, but we will rebuild!" he said defiantly.

Several people agreed with feeling.

"I hope your colleagues agree with you," I said, "because there is no future here. Okay, you people know everything that we know. Fill your groups in. Tomorrow morning at 0900, we have a general meeting to finalize abandonment plans for Luna Base. Command staff meets in my quarters an hour before."

XI

A Hard Decision

"I think we have found safe haven for every soul in this base," I began after coffee had been issued to all. "We now have detailed maps of the most habitable areas and willing human settlements. Most are in outlying areas with little contamination. Most of these lie in the extreme latitudes, north, and south, some of the remote deserts and a number of remote pacific islands. Some of these are uninhabited. Now, survivors may be attempting to reach them. But few will know about them, fewer still will have the means to take a sea voyage, and fewer still will survive it."

"With people being people, everyone is going to want to go somewhere different," Wes observed, "which would be a good thing, as large groups appearing in an area will stress local resources more. We should all scrounge the crew cabins for clothes. Most of these people only have the uniforms their wearing."

I nodded, "That is a good idea. We will list the safe areas and let them choose where they want to live."

Cole spoke again, "What will we use as currency? Should we take things to trade, maybe?"

I shook my head, "I doubt that there is any currency worth more than its value as kindling now. I don't think we have much that doesn't require power cells. There might be something on some of the other ships. Its hand tools, rope, and know how that will be the most valuable. It's carry-on luggage only for this final trip."

Rachael asked, "Do we need to restrict the size of the groups from the start to family size or smaller?"

"Depends on the location," I answered. "That is factored into the maps based on available resources. We don't want to add to an Eco system that's above fifty percent capacity. They will all need room to grow."

"Everyone had better pick someone they like," Rachael said, "for they could be the only friendly faces we see for years," she concluded with a grim look on her face.

"We have a few weeks, but the sooner we make that first drop, the better," I observed.

Silence gripped the table as the enormity of the task ahead of everyone on the base took hold.

I broke the silence, "If no one has any other questions, I think we should call everyone to the central lecture hall now and get started."

The others nodded, and Rachael went to call the meeting.

Twenty minutes later, I was standing at a podium with a handful of notes and three hundred seventy-two pairs of eyes on me. For someone who had dedicated his life to working in the shadows, it was not a particularly pleasant experience. I steeled myself and cleared my throat.

"Ladies and Gentlemen, our species has been dealt a vicious blow. I know that every single one of you have lost loved ones... family, friends, and crewmates. Even the others of our own kind we once called 'enemy' are now to be mourned. But the time for memorial is not now. Things are bad. The worst they have ever been. And it's not over."

I glanced at Rachael and an image appeared on the huge screen behind me.

I continued, "What you are seeing is the entirety of our food supply. We can last two months, or four on half rations. There is zero possibility of generating sufficient food here. This base has always had weekly supply runs."

There was dead silence.

"Our only option is to return to Earth," I stated.

A murmur passed through the crowd.

"But we have a plan. A plan to give you every possible chance to live out the rest of your lives as you choose. You have all been provided with maps showing the areas with the highest likelihood of establishing a permanent population. These have all been chosen with mild climate in mind to facilitate food availability. Every group will be provided with one hard copy military survival guide to aid you in finding food and water, building shelter, basic first aid and more. Every group will get a med-kit issued to the most qualified.

"We will drop you all off in the location of your choosing in small groups. I'm not going to sugar coat this. Things are going to be rough at first. You may struggle to find food and shelter, but remember we are still the lucky ones."

A hand rose near the edge of the room.

"Yes?" I asked.

"Are other locations banned, or can we choose outside the temperate zone?" a stout young man asked.

"What did you have in mind?" I inquired.

"I am Inuit. My family still lives in the same remote village on Prince Patrick Island, many still use the old ways." he said.

I gave him a firm look. "I hope you find your family safe when you get there, son," I said with a nod. I turned back to the room and continued, "Anyone else who feels better suited to another location is welcome to inquire afterward. We will also be posting lists of the previous station personnel, with their height, weight, sex, and locker number. A bit macabre, I know, but we all have a need for clothes. The next ones you get you will probably make yourself. Don't take more than you can carry. You don't escape a disaster complete with a luggage cart. When you have decided on your location, enter it at any public terminal and be ready to go at any time, as the weather will dictate landing dates and times. Now, if there are no more questions, I will see each of you on our final flight together. Best of luck to you all," I closed.

People began filing out with a handful moving toward Rachael at the front of the room.

The next few days fell into a routine. Every morning beginning with a weather report, and culminating in fewer voices echoing in the corridors of the once crowded base.

On each drop, we landed near a village, successfully made contact with the locals, and in moments we were back in the air. Not one village had heard from the outside world since the attack. All of their technology was fried in the EMP, just as the scans had indicated. There were still some wind powered craft on the islands and these would become valuable fishing vessels as populations began to grow I surmised, but with little in the way of tools or the tooling to make tools, it was going to be like reinventing the wheel.

With three hundred and seventy three souls on this base, this could take a few days, depending on weather patterns.

I was sitting alone in the corner of the galley gazing out at the stars when Rachael walked up.

"May I join you, Colonel?" she asked.

I smiled and gestured to the opposite seat, "What can I do for you?"

She stared at me with a suspicious look, "I have thre hundred and seventy-two destination selections in front of me," nodding at her display, "but the headcount is three hundred seventy-three. What do you make of this?"

"You caught me!" I said with a guilty chuckle. "I'm not going back to Earth. Hell, I haven't spent a week planet-side since I graduated the academy."

Rachael's face softened, "I had my eye on an atoll northeast of New Zealand. I was hoping you might enjoy a tropical climate... with me."

I had never taken the time to look at her as a woman before. She was very pretty with piercing blue eyes, peering out from behind a regulation fleet haircut that was several weeks overgrown. For a fleeting second, I was tempted.

I looked down and shook my head, "I'm neither farmer nor colonist. The term marooned comes immediately to mind. Men are less vital than women when rebuilding a species, you know!" The memory of the alien technology permeating my very cells was very prominent in my mind right at that moment. It had been a long time since I stopped and thought about my microscopic robot problem. For all I knew, sex with me could be deadly. Literally. I had no idea if these things were transmissible, nor what might happen to anyone contaminated.

She smiled and placed her hand on mine. I withdrew, "No. I'm sorry. I can't..."

"No, it's my fault. I thought..." she said then turned and walked swiftly away.

I couldn't tell her. I was the only one who knew about the nanos. Until I knew more about them, I had to assume I was a danger. I couldn't risk turning the remnants of mankind into cyborgs. I had no choice but to try to find out who created the technology. I had an uneasy feeling it would be a long time before I see Earth again.

George Olafson and Herb Pickard spent their last week helping me to modify the Phantom so that I could operate most of her controls from the center seat. I was amazed at how much they were able to automate. She should serve me fine for the task ahead, I thought.

As days passed the Luna Base population dwindled to the last few, soon to be, pioneers. These were people I had come to call friends. A rarity in my line of work. For the first time in my life, goodbye was hard. We had decided it would be best to destroy the base when we left with the final group, eliminating any possibility of a future trap, or some alien deciding it would make a great hideout.

The Glasgow crew had decided to stick together, and they had chosen Tonga as their new home. They were the last humans to set foot upon the moon.

As Rachael entered the ship, she paused in the entryway, turned and looked back at the empty station, silent except for a chorus of mechanical hums. "Well, it was fun while it lasted," she said sadly, as the door sealed.

There was barely a sound in the Phantom as the base disappeared in a flash under the gaze of her plasma cannons.

Later, we silently overflew the archipelago in the darkness The Phantom banked sharply and came to rest in the same clearing.

I walked out with the crew and we laid their meager belongings on the ground. I turned and looked at each one of them. I was surprised by the connection I felt to them.

"Mr. Cole!" I said, "All we've been through and I still don't know your first name!"

He laughed, "Perseus. Now you know why I never tell anyone! You take care of yourself, Mac," he said as he grasped my hand firmly.

"George," I began, "we wouldn't have made it this far without you! You all did a remarkable job under unprecedented circumstances."

"It was a pleasure working with you, Mac."

I then came to Rachael. She was standing at attention, but when our eyes met she burst out, "Ah hell!" she said as she lunged forward and wrapped her arms around me, "I'm not in the military anymore," she whispered before she kissed me.

My gaze lingered on the island disappearing into the distance on the aft display. I shook myself back to reality and entered a course to the one location I might find a clue to who created the nano technology... Mars.

*****

Kvaaa'tu stirred and another complex tune floated through the air. The translator flashed urgently as its processors strained.

"Kvaaa'tu interrupts data acquisition. Kvaaa'tu proposes continuation of data stream in four cycles," the dispassionate voice of the translator finally said.

"Accepted. I will return here in four cycles to continue data stream"

XII

Endless Space

The stars moved by very slowly on gravity drive. It was nothing like the old sci-fi movies. I find my mind drifts easily staring out into space. It's as if I can hear the universe's thoughts. I guess reality sometimes intersects with our imaginations, but is frequently more mundane. In reality, the distance between stars is far more than the mind can comprehend, so it conveniently perceives it as boredom for humans. I had another ten hours to travel at effectively one thousand times light speed to reach Gamma Centauri.

Earth's closest neighbor, Proxima Centauri, was more than thirty-six hours away from my old home world at this speed. My name is Robert MacKesson. It had taken me over a year to get out to the Frontier after the almost complete destruction of the human race. It is an infrequent treat to pass a star system even in the much denser parts of the galaxy, and once you get underway, the computer does everything else. It gives an excellent impression of being under house arrest.

I had left two days previous on my way to my second meeting with the Vajhi historian, Kvaaa'tu. I rather enjoyed hearing the strange being speak, his language, and speech reminded me of the sounds of the Theremin we built in grade school science class. My translator must have dreaded the load on its processor. I could swear it gets a snippy tone after talking to him for a while.

There is nothing much to do but read, eat, and sleep during these times, that is, when I have nothing else to work on. This time I chose the latter.

An alarm pulled me from a deep sleep. I yawned and got to my feet, triggering the lights to brighten to day mode. I tapped a button on my battle computer and the alarm silenced as its cause appeared on my virtual interface. Comms traffic within one parsec. I learned early on in my basic training not to be- conspicuous in any way if you didn't control the situation. In an infinite universe, you can never be sure of controlling any situation, so a low profile becomes a way of life if you want said life to continue. The Phantom's gravity drive was detectable at that speed from a little under a parsec away because of the distortion of the warped space. I always liked to know who's in the neighborhood before they noticed me, just in case their motives weren't benign.

I grabbed a food pack and headed to the bridge. An image of the local star group slowly rotated on the central holographic display with a point highlighted with a pulsating red circle.

It was an excellent time to real-world test the new database I was getting from Kvaaa'tu. I entered the encryption key for the first portion of the data. The display flickered and reappeared with hundreds of labels and data codes on what must have been every rock larger than half a kilometer within four parsecs in every direction.

The red circle had landed perfectly on an asteroid field a few light-years away. I zoomed in on the image on the signal origin, and was surprised at the detail of the database. Many shapes and features were clearly defined on the image. I touched a small symbol that was floating among the drifting asteroids. A label appeared in place of the icon. A second later, the words were translated into their closest English equivalent.

"Mining Colony. Botreiki Consortium," it said, followed by a long list of elements they supplied.

This could be a very useful tool for someone in my precarious position.

I altered my course to stay well outside their sensor range and continued on my way toward my rendezvous with Kvaaa'tu. When you have, or in fact are, a rare item, it's never good to telegraph your movements. Shortly after my arrival in the Frontier, I had the distinct displeasure of being told by an alien to wait while they determined whether I was sentient, or had escaped from their food stores.

The small pair of dots I had been pursuing for the last two days was looming larger on the forward display. Gamma Centauri is a binary system, which is favored by the ship building industry. The Kree have a huge space dock complex at the LaGrange point between the two stars, providing them with staggering amounts of free energy for processing ore into ships' hulls. This of course brings in all the support industries to keep the workers fed and entertained. It had inadvertently become one of the prime trading centers of the Frontier. It was a cantina in this sprawling complex that was my destination. The entire complex was heavily armed to discourage fights from breaking out between species. It was well known that their policy was to destroy both sides in any violent exchange to protect the hundreds of thousands who lived and worked there. One stray shot and an entire section could decompress. It worked, as armed exchanges were rare.

As I rounded the nearer star, the Kree docks came into view. The color-coded sections swept silently by as I headed for the brightly colored and flashy entertainment complex. There weren't too many desires that you couldn't fulfill there in the clubs and hologram suites. By Earth standards, it would be considered immoral, but in an infinite universe, such concepts as morality can have completely different meanings. A common courtesy to one race can be a vile insult to another. This took some getting used to.

I rounded the entertainment section and approached the landing bay. There was a jolt as tractor beams locked onto the Phantom, guiding her through a maze of gantries and ships to an open dock. There it gently pulled her into place as the magnetic moorings clamped onto the hull. I stood from the command chair and stretched. Thanks to the nanos, I was able to walk around in the station without a breathing apparatus. The individual café's not only had varying themes and décor as Earth had once had, but they also catered to specific clientele by offering the gravity and peculiar gas mixture of many different worlds. This made it vitally important to be able to read and understand the markings on every door, lest you find yourself in the hot, sulfuric climate of one of the intensely volcanic planets.

I pulled up a map on my battle computer and the station appeared, hovering transparently in front of my eye. I picked up my jacket and headed toward the airlock.

The gravity plating in the common areas was set to about point seven g by Earth standards, making loads easier to carry, but keeping enough weight for stability.

I set out at a brisk pace heading toward The Magic Window bar where Kvaaa'tu would arrive at the agreed time, not one second before, or after. The Magic Window had an interesting hook. Sensors did a superficial scan of patron's brain, and the computers took actual events from your life and embellished them into comedic holographic shows on your table. This aspect didn't appeal to me, but their food was tasty, and their drinks weren't toxic to me. I had learned long ago not to ask what the food was if my battle computer said, it was safe to eat. That information rarely improved the meal.

Four kilometers of corridors later, I entered the Magic Window and found an isolated table against the wall. This place seemed oppressive, like much of the rest if the facility. I had always put this down to the total lack of windows. When you are floating between two binary stars, having a window could blind everyone in the room.

I sat down half an hour before Kvaaa'tu was to arrive and ordered the most appealing image on the menu, which, I hoped, would turn out to be dinner. The food came almost impossibly fast. I pulled a thin probe from my battle computer and inserted it into the dish the insectoid waiter had delivered. A second's analysis and the response was non-toxic. I sampled it cautiously. It was not bad at all. It was a pastry filled with some kind of meat and vegetables, oddly similar to potpies on Earth, even in the respect that you were never completely sure what was inside most of them.

I finished my meal and sat sipping on some hot tu-chuk. It was the closest thing I had found to coffee. It was not too distant from what I remember on Earth, but more of a sweet, nutty flavor. From the image of the advertisements, it appeared to be made from a fungus.

Kvaaa'tu appeared exactly when he said he would.

The soft, flowing tones of his voice floated across the table and the translator began to flash furiously. A few moments later the translation broke the silence, "Salutations MacKesson. It is pleasing to continue our exchange. Kvaaa'tu is ready to begin."

I smiled and said, "It pleases me to continue our exchange, and your star data is impressive. MacKesson extends complements and appreciation."

The translator flickered away as it converted my words to a sublime melody.

I sat back and let my mind drift the hundred and thirty odd light-years back to the still smoldering remains of my home planet...

XIII

The Search for a Clue

The Phantom banked low in the Mars sky as I circled over the dark crater, which marked the only visible trace of the secret base. The energy it took to destroy this fortified base under half a mile of rock and ice was inconceivable. The surface had been liquefied, and thermal scans showed the surface of the crater was still hot almost two months after the attack by the Izars had devastated humanity.

The Izars were a space fairing race when mankind was still working out how to make spears. In a scant ten thousand years, man had gone from stone axes and a sky full of mysterious gods, to reaching the stars and trying to understand the very makeup of the universe. From that timescale, one can't even imagine some of the discoveries made by the races a billion years older.

However, the human exploration instinct carries with it a level of arrogance. A sense that anywhere we go we will bring freedom and enlightenment to the natives. That was when we were the big boys in our little neighborhood.

I pulled up the track of my previous escape from the devastated facility, and located the canyon, which led to the docking bay. The bay itself was too small to accommodate the Phantom, but the canyon was wide enough in places to land. A few moments later, she touched down lightly in a cloud of red dust.

Winter was approaching in this hemisphere and temperature could easily be minus one hundred centigrade, near the limit for the planetary enviro suit on board. I did a quick scan of the outside conditions as the fast moving mars winds swept the clouds of dust away down the canyon. The temperature was much warmer than it should be this time of year. The residual energy of the attack must have warmed the entire area. Radiation was well above normal, but within tolerance for a short time. Success or failure of this mission would be determined well before the danger level had been reached.

A few minutes later, I was standing once again in the same canyon that had served as my escape route after the attack. My mind drifted back to the corridor with Anna Stotfold as she pressed the hypodermic injector against my neck. She had no idea that there would be no earth government remaining to receive the microscopic army of nanobots. Not to mention that there were not enough people left on Earth to fill a sports stadium, much less retaliate. That left me with some nagging problems. What could they do long term, could they be transmitted, and what would this transmission do to the new host? I clearly could not risk infecting the remaining fragment of humanity with the self-replicating machines.

That thought brought me back to reality and my purpose for coming there. This was my only lead to find out how to remove these things. I was sure they used crystal memory in the central core backup. It was standard in all military research facilities as a record of what went wrong in case of a catastrophic failure. Crystal memory was impervious to the electromagnetic pulse of weapons, so should have survived the attack.

The bigger question was how to get to it, if it were even accessible. Most of the upper section appeared to be obliterated when I inspected it before, but the memory core was always put a distance from the operational areas and its location classified. It was not on the map of the base I had downloaded into my battle computer my last time here.

I made my way up the rover path to the still open bay door and shined a beam of light inside. With the addition of a few tons of windblown dust, it looked the same as when I left. I made my way through the inner door and started up the spiral toward where I had regained consciousness after the attack.

I had noticed before that the lower end of the spiral passage had been widened about fifty meters up from the rover bay. This made no sense unless it had to be wider to accommodate moving some kind of equipment. The only problem with that was there were no other openings onto this corridor until the top. I walked slowly up the corridor scanning the walls. Here and there, cracks had opened in the coating, which kept the rock stable after the tunneling to build the base.

As I neared the end of the wider portion of the corridor, my scanner showed a drop in density of the wall. This had to be the way the memory core equipment was brought in. It was cheaper to make the large tunnel direct from the outside with the added benefit of reduced susceptibility to shockwaves if there were any explosive accidents in the labs. The personnel entrance would have been in a high security location on the upper levels. My chances of finding a path that way were infinitesimal. I switched scanning modes and was able to read a void about four feet behind the faux rock.

I quickly returned to the Phantom and removed an explosive charge from the weapons locker. A short time later, I placed it in the center of the artificial section of the corridor, and activated the charge. I retreated to the outer rover bay and triggered the charge. A high crack followed by a low rumble carried through the thin air followed by a cloud of dust.

The blast had revealed a long curving tunnel as wide as the corridor outside. At the end of the tunnel, a small spiral staircase disappeared upward opposite a massive titanium door. The power circuits for the door were dead, but the computer itself seemed intact. I pulled a portable power cell from my bag and connected it to the supplemental power port on the lock and it glowed to life. I extended a thin optical cable from my battle computer and interfaced with it. I was in luck. My security credentials had been logged before the attack, so it still recognized my clearance.

An audible click echoed through the stone chamber as the locking mechanism released allowing me to spin the wheel on the manual release. Even in the low gravity of mars, the massive door took some effort to open. I disconnected the power cell and entered the darkened chamber. The beam of my light illuminated a circular room ringed with electronics. It was sparsely furnished as maintenance teams were the only ones who ever visited the cores

155

routinely. I placed the power cell on a console and connected a pair of floodlights to it and the shades of gray resolved into an ordinary looking computer room. An inspection of the crystal memory unit confirmed what I had feared. Its power demands were more than every power cell I had. I could not beam microwave power that far through rock. I would have to run a line in from ships power to have any chance of recovering the data.

A hundred meter power cable wasn't going to appear before me anytime soon. Perhaps the personnel tunnel from the core would still reach one of the main corridors or provide access to some place I might be able to scavenge some cabling. I picked up my bag and headed back out to the spiral stairs to begin the half-kilometer vertical climb from this remote corner of the complex.

Soon, the way was blocked by a wall of black stone. The crust above the base had been liquefied by the sheer power of the Izar weapons, and lava had flowed down any opening provided, whether natural or man-made. I could feel heat still radiating from the mass. There would be no digging through this.

I backtracked to the memory core and exited to the rover corridor, but headed this time further on, back to the shuttle bay that had allowed my ingress after being trapped on the surface.

Near the top lay the first corpse that I had seen since my return. Frozen in time at the minute of the attack. They couldn't be left this way.

Making my way past and on to the shuttle bay, I quickly found what I came for. Several coils of cable were stacked against the wall, addressed to the server room. A short length of rope secured two of them together and I slung them over my shoulder.

A short time later, I was back at the ship. It would take a couple of hours to reverse the ship's shore power couplings to provide a feed and run the cables back to the memory core, and another hour or so to download the data.

It was almost sunset, and already dark in the canyon. Hunger convinced me it was time to call it a day. There was nothing time critical for me anymore. I returned to the Phantom for dinner and a restless night.

With the dawn came a spectacular red sunrise. There was a dust storm far over the horizon that was lifting the dry, pulverized stone high into Mars' atmosphere. In all the chaos and destruction, the simple, unerring beauty of nature remained unstoppable.

The sun was high in the sky when the last connection was made and the memory core glowed with life. They took an immense amount of power. Gamma lasers nudged molecules of large diamonds to store binary data directly in the microcrystals. Theoretically, it took temperatures over $4,600°$ kelvin to destroy the data. As long as you had all the pieces, data could be recovered from an exploded crystal at a rate of one hundred percent. This one had only sustained superficial damage during the attack. The crystals themselves were unharmed. Systems had recorded magnitude eight shockwaves before power supplies had been cut.

I copied the entire contents of the archive to my battle computer, then deleted the engineering, design, and classified archives from the core.

"Computer," I said into the microphone in my helmet, "Record the following statement and set for autoplay protocol upon power on.

The computer blinked compliance.

I cleared my throat and began, "Here before you stands the remains of the dreams of your ancestors. Before you were born, mankind had already touched the stars. We had knowledge before we had the wisdom to use it, and paid a terrible price. If you have made it this far again, you face the same danger. Take the data in this device and use it to guide your actions. Learn from our mistakes. Forgive us for what we did in the name of King and Country. Message end."

As the power coupling twisted in my hand, the complex machine went dark. With any luck, it would awaken again one day.

The next five days were spent poring over the data about the nanos until my eyes screamed and digging graves for the base personnel found so far. On day four, I backtracked to the fissure in which I had awakened after the attack. I moved

Robbie and all others I could find back out to the gravesite I had chosen.

Having time for a more thorough search this time uncovered several more bodies, including Anna Stotfold, the Base Director. Her hand still held the hypodermic injector that had kept me alive. Her small body was the lightest of all.

Seven days after I had arrived, the Phantom broke the empty silence of Mars as she lifted and banked over the landscape. The Martian sunset silhouetted twenty-four mounds of stones on a rise overlooking a vast plain. I angled her nose skyward and watched the ground drop away in the aft viewer as the sky ahead turned inky black.

XIV

Goodbye Sol

The records had given me more questions than answers. I had step-by-step plans to build the damn nanos, but nothing mentioning uninstalling, or deactivating them.

There was more than one alien technology involved here. The atomic manipulation technology was utterly incomprehensible to me. It was acquired in a deal with a race listed only as Species 112811. I could find no other reference to them in any of my archives.

The micro-replicator was only listed as outsourced, but the technical notes mentioned a request being routed to a Xihji trader. The Xihji were notorious black marketers. They were banned from Earth surface travel after an influx of dangerous and prohibited goods. It seemed that every government believed in the "Do as I say, not as I do." philosophy.

The Xihji were a good starting point. The trader mentioned was Yuud Masar. I had booked passage with him on earlier covert missions. He had a small asteroid mining operation near Alpha Proxima that he used as a front to smuggle stolen goods. He was a shrewd businessman, like most of his people, but understood little about the technical aspects of anything he moved. However, maybe he could be persuaded to look the other way while I perused his files. It was a beginning.

"Computer: Plot and implement standard course to Alpha Proxima. Alert me at Alpha Proxima heliopause minus ten minutes," I said to the computer.

"Course computed and implemented," came the reply.

That one command gave me the next day and a half free to learn about my new nano-companions.

As the Phantom tore through the vast emptiness of I combed terabytes of information looking for the rare useful crumb hidden in the monotonous technical logs. Finally, a coherent picture began to emerge.

The nanos had completed testing and were being prepared for a human trial when the Izari crisis erupted. These blank nanos imprinted with the host genome within moments of being introduced. This gave them the perfect map for repairing damage to the body at the cellular level. Over time bringing the host to well above average human strength.

I had noticed my muscle tone had not succumbed to low gravity atrophy despite being unable to spend the necessary time in the gym. Perhaps this wasn't all bad.

As Mars had proven, their ability to break the CO_2 bond, providing themselves with carbon and the host with O_2 was a complete success. I would be okay in any atmosphere that had oxygen anywhere in its chemical makeup. However, the nanos weren't capable of changing the atoms themselves.

None of IP's finest scientists understood the processor, which gave the microscopic machines

163

near droid sophistication. They described it as having a computer core that was larger than the nano itself, extending in a quantum flux to parallel dimensions

They could modify the sensory organs, eye lenses, and eardrums bringing all of the hosts senses back to child-aged sharpness or better.

They regulated body chemistry removing waste in the form of a much denser urine, resulting in extended survival capability without water.

They could neutralize any poisons that they recognize as a threat

Potential lifespan: Greater than one millennia

That point sent a shudder through me. IP Industries wanted armies with this enhancement! The briefing that we had been given had mentioned nothing more than increased stamina and resistance to biological agents in the troops.

The Achilles heel of non-reversible augmentation had been proven before in covert genetic manipulation programs in the late 21st century. When you enhance a man into a superhuman killing machine, you have to consider what happens when said super soldier doesn't want to be a soldier anymore. An orderly society can't permit people who are genetically or psychologically predisposed to overpower opposition free movement in public.

The answer they found in the last century resulted in the unfortunate volunteers being hunted down as "insane terrorists from a neurological weapon experiment" gone wrong. The truth was less glamorous, but more bloody. A single platoon of fifteen men was enhanced genetically and with cybernetic implants. Once they got to realize their full potential, they began to resent being ordered around by inferior old men. It took an entire division of battle-hardened troops to kill them. Casualties were high.

Now IP had been planning to create the perfect war machine from the inside out. Hundreds or thousands of super strong soldiers, capable of self-healing, with lifespans over a thousand years would have probably been as devastating as the Izar attack.

165

It was a moot point though, as from everything I had seen so far that there was no imaginable enhancement that could have saved us from the Izar.

I didn't get a single survivors' report mentioning the huge ship suffering any damage whatsoever.

When your opponent is so far advanced from you that you can't even understand what happened, a change in approach is required.

Since I was exiled from my own world for the time being, I may as well begin gathering intelligence about our enemy. I opened a new file on my battle computer's Enemy Analysis application. It would compile any new information I acquired as time progressed, as well as scan the Mars Base core memory data heuristically for any reference to the Izar or sudden deep space threats for the last month of operation. Over time it could extrapolate enemy force size, strength and predict intent with a better than chance accuracy.

However, considering the current state of the human race, a retaliatory strike in following next century was absurdly remote. Therefore, my top priority would remain getting rid of, or gaining control of the nanobots.

A few hours later, I had decided to get some sleep.

"Computer, route all alerts to my battle computer until I return," I said as I rose and started toward the door.

A voice replied, "Aye, aye. Changes complete."

"Lights," I said, and when the lights winked out, I was shocked to realize I could see much better than should be possible at this light level. Some things seemed to emit light. I looked at my hands, as they seemed to be glowing as well!

"Lights!" The effect vanished. I turned the lights off again, and walked down the corridor to the weapons locker and pulled out a night vision torch. At the touch of its switch, the room was flooded with light. This light was infrared, and should be invisible to humans!

Apparently, the nanobots were still working on my remodel. I could really see the lure of this.

There had been many missions where I would have traded my right arm for this ability. Moreover, I suspected it might prove to be useful many times before I make it home.

I turned and walked slowly to my cabin marveling at the patterns of heat being emitted by various things around the ship. "This will take some getting used to!" I thought as I retired for the day.

A few hours later, I awakened to the beeping of my battle computer. It had drawn some conclusions from the Izar data.

I sprang lightly to my feet. Since the nanos took care of my physique, I had set the grav plating down to sixty percent. I was fortunate that the Phantom had this new technology. Most of the deep space Earth craft had still used rotational gravity.

The Phantom was obviously a prototype from her IPS X1 construction code. 'X1' always designated experimental testing stage one. This meant that she was getting ready for her shakedown cruise when she was inbound to Ganymede, disguised as the light freighter, Glasgow.

On my way to the bridge, I grabbed a meal bar from a dispenser and breakfasted as I walked.

As I entered the bridge, the soft glowing shapes of the equipment were suddenly replaced by their normal image as the lights came up.

"Computer, open battle computer's analysis of enemy weapon on 3D display," I said aloud.

Images appeared slowly rotating showing a weapon impact site with various shadings indicating different types of radiation. I read the summary with stunned amazement. The alien weapon somehow destabilized the atomic bonds of matter at the target point starting a fusion reaction. The readings indicated that the reaction had blasted almost a hundred meters into the bedrock of the crater in Paris.

This had to be a horribly efficient weapon if the actual destruction is all done by the target itself!

We had been fighting with the technological equivalent of sticks and stones.

The beep of the navigation control brought me out of thought. I was nearing Proxima Centauri.

Scans of the system ahead indicated a number of ships had passed by recently at high gravity drive. The Xihji seemed to be doing a brisk business at their new location. They had built this outpost on a large asteroid after they had been banned from Earth. It quickly became the liquor store in the next town for the space dogs, as freighter crews were known.

Almost everyone knew 'someone' who knew 'someone' who could get any vice you could imagine. Banning something people want invariably creates a thriving black-market. It's a simple premise that politicians frequently used to create an artificial need for additional law enforcement.

By having many overlapping departments and jurisdictions, the rulers had armed officers almost everywhere. Even though they all had different structures and leaders, all of those leaders invariably answer to one person or group. The covert dictatorships were the most successful in Earth's history. The people didn't mind being ruled as long as they did know they were being ruled. Looking back at each example over the ages, historians had simply followed the money back to the true rulers.

That premise had served me well in dealing with hundreds of countries and dozens of alien races over my career. It seemed that most interstellar races had the same innate instinct as man for putting themselves first, whether by nature or as a learned defense in the Frontier.

I disengaged the gravity drive and activated stealth flight mode. This masked all external radiation with the exception of ion drive exhaust, which dissipates quickly.

I wanted to see who the other guests at the Xihji outpost were, before I announced my presence.

The outpost was essentially an interstellar barge that had been anchored to the asteroid with an enviro plant. They didn't do permanent installations for just a drive thru business. Yuud was a particularly thrifty merchant, preferring profit to his or his employees comfort. Only his ship's captains had cabins of their own. The crew was left to fashion their own sleeping arrangements amongst the cargo. A dangerous prospect with an inexperienced pilot, due to sudden movements shifting the cargo. Yuud had a lot of turnover.

This outpost would surely be dismantled when news got to him, if it hadn't already. If he had not received the news, it could give me just the leverage I needed to get a look at his files.

XV

The Next Piece of the Puzzle

Yuud Masar was seedy, even by Xihji standards. He was the one who fleeced the primitive cultures that the more ethical traders avoided.

There didn't appear to be any other ships about the outpost at the time.

"Computer, open channel to outpost," I said.

A tone indicated compliance.

"This is the Ear…" I hesitated, "This is the vessel Phantom, requesting permission to dock."

A moment later a thick voice returned, "Permission granted. Access dock protocol on the channel to follow."

A few minutes later, I was face to face with the Xihji, Yuud Masar.

"Mac! Mac, Yuud old and dear friend, how pleased it makes Yuud to see you! It has been many Earth Days and no ships! But now Mac comes!" he dripped.

I gave him a tight smile, "Yuud. How's the black-market treating you these days?"

An almost comical look of horror exploded across his face. "Yuud? No, Mac! Yuud doesn't deal with that scum!"

"Relax! I'm not here for you. You always bring us the nice toys. I'm here to look into a missing shipment," I lied. "It was a very tiny cargo."

His baggy yellow face brightened at the news that IP didn't have an issue with him. He nodded knowingly, "You mean the…"

"Yes. There was only fifty percent of the agreed amount in the container. I'm here to collect what is owed. Now do I begin collecting here, or do you have a suggestion of someone else who bears the responsibility, Mister Masar?" I said with an intent gaze.

"No, Mac! Mac and IP are good customer! Yuud would not cheat you! Yuud had no way of knowing. They so tiny! Yuud tell supplier when comes next," he gasped, wheezing loudly.

I shook my head, "No, Yuud. I will see your contact personally. Where is your supplier? We are getting ready to place a big order with you, Yuud. We must know you can deliver," I paused, "I like you, Yuud. You always help a guy out with hard to get items. I would rather see someone else take the fall so we can continue to do business. Can we do that, Yuud?" I asked.

He looked a bit apprehensive and then said, "Yuud says yes. If, you never tell Yuud broke sacred word!"

"Yuud, I can promise you that I will not hurt your reputation in any way," I said earnestly.

He shuffled off to his computer. A few seconds later, my battle computer made a tiny beep in my ear indicating a transmission received. I pulled up the info invisibly on my virtual interface and quickly looked it over. It seemed legitimate.

Yuud shuffled back over. "Is that good for Mac and IP? Look! It's okay?" he said.

I smiled again, "Yuud! I trust you! This will do."

As I walked in the direction of the Phantom, I paused again, "Oh, Yuud," I said over my shoulder, "Earth was destroyed by the Izari. You're out of business here."

Back aboard ship, I moved the Phantom away from the outpost to a large asteroid a few hundred thousand kilometers distant, and gently made contact in the microgravity. The rehydrator beeped its completion of my dinner as I got to work on the Xihji data. He had gotten the nanos from a rogue trader who worked out of a bazaar on a world about sixty light-years distant orbiting Iota Centauri, also known as The Thieves Market.

I looked at the name and wondered if there had been a data glitch. It seemed that Wenvin Wo was the automatic translator's phonetic equivalent in English.

I wondered if I would ever get used to all of the bizarre sounds of the multitude of alien languages, variety of speech organs, and methods of communicating.

Without the translation technology, mankind had no hope of ever being part of the greater galaxy. We simply didn't have the brainpower to learn the complex languages of the older races. Without common frames of reference, it would have taken decades to decipher some of the languages. Some would be impossible due to thought alien processes more complex that we could begin to understand.

Wo had an entry in my IP files. The corporation had used this particular trader before. According to the record, he was more of a thief for hire.

He was from an insectoid race that had been conquered by another a few centuries ago. The few that escaped had become vagabonds, following opportunity across the galaxy.

Settlers were rarely welcomed on any planet, and every attempt by the Prdynon to colonize had failed. Most eventually return to their nomadic ways, relocating as easy resources dwindled.

The Prdynon funded this lifestyle by specializing in contraband and goods from unknown sources. They claimed to be exempt from conventional law as people without a land. From what we had learned, this strategy was only effective when the Prdynon had a decided advantage against an already inferior opponent.

"Computer: Plot a course to Iota Centauri," I said aloud.

The computer beeped compliance and an image appeared with a blue line disappearing into the star field.

The quiet of the ship was broken by a proximity alert. It was probably just one of Yuud Masar's ships arriving, but decades of training caused me to pull up the image anyway.

I was greeted by a ship design that I had never seen before. It was larger than the Phantom by several times and looked like an opaque, dark blue, shard of glass. The ship was holding at a distance of five hundred meters from the outpost, the data display said. I didn't want to give away my position by using any type of active scans, thus patience may be the more valuable tool here.

I watched with curiosity, waiting for some sort of docking craft to emerge. The sensors detected a sudden energy signature, and then it was gone.

I analyzed the spike to see if it contained some form of communication. Nothing.

As the asteroid slowly rotated, the craft maintained exactly the same position relative to the outpost, and the next few seconds brought the alien ship into full sunlight. Somehow, its featureless shape looked even more menacing even though there were no obvious weapons. Just a smooth, deep blue shape with no apparent surface features.

The strange ship had only been illuminated for a few moments when the computer indicated a possible database match.

I pulled up the reference with interest. It wasn't in the ship's database, but rather in the data from the memory core on Mars. The same deep blue color flashed on the 3D display. It was a different, much larger ship, but undoubtedly from the same maker judging by the sharp lines and striking color.

I looked at the image reference data. This image was captured less than three minutes before Mars Colony Alpha was destroyed.

This was an Izar ship! This was the first time I had seen one of the ships that destroyed my entire planet.

The Jovian attack had been so distant that the ship itself was not in visual range when the Glasgow had detected the attack and ran, and the ragtag condition of the survivors ships had offered no useful data either.

I was momentarily overcome with a feeling of rage. I stormed over to the command chair and stopped. I took a deep breath as I checked my emotions.

Going up against an enemy ship of unknown strength alone would be tantamount to suicide.

Again, there was an energy spike from the vessel. A few seconds later, the vessel broke its delicate orbit and headed into open space. I kept every sensor trained on her as she pulled clear of the asteroids.

In a blink, the Izar ship disappeared. As their gravity drive distorted space and hurled the ship across the void, it flashed a microsecond burst of radiation. That mixture of x-rays, gamma rays, and Hawking radiation would give me a nice look at their propulsion system after analysis.

I sat down and powered up the Phantom. Another visit to my "dear friend" Yuud Masar was in order.

"What was his connection to the Izar?" was the first of many questions I had for him.

Discretion is usually the better part of valor.

"More lives have been won and lost covertly than on the battlefield!" I could still hear my old ops instructor's catch phrase. I guess it was true. Back then.

I fired the pressure thrusters and began drifting toward the Xihji outpost. They were essentially over-powered, extended capacity maneuvering thrusters. The acceleration was minimal, but they would get you up to a considerable speed over a distance. In Black Ops, we used them to get a craft up to speed and pass silently by the target until deployment of whatever asset required. The one on the Phantom was much more advanced than the rudimentary devices we had in those days. In either case, it was as quiet as we primitive humans had managed thus far, and tediously slow.

XVI

A Gruesome Discovery

Silently and swiftly, I passed through the dark passages in the Xihji outpost. I was clad in a Special Services tactical suit. The material was designed to reflect no light from any angle. In a dark area, it was near to invisibility.

I had passed a few of Yuud's employees, all of whom seemed to be hurriedly loading handcarts full of items from inventory.

As I approached Yuud's office area things were unusually quiet. There was only one light on, and it appeared to be coming from Yuud's office itself.

The sliver of light was all that my nanobot-enhanced vision needed to see every detail of my surroundings clearly.

There were several desks with computer displays arranged in rows across the long room. A number of chairs were on their sides. Something big had gone on here. An eight-fingered hand protruded lifelessly from under a desk.

I moved silently down the passage toward the light. Pausing briefly outside the door, my enhanced ears heard only the low hum of power feeds.

The door swung open to a light touch, revealing a horrific scene. Someone had been very perturbed with Yuud Masar. He had been strapped to his desk and sliced with a surgical laser. The laser cauterized as it cut preventing him from bleeding out. The expression on his face said he was alive for it. Someone had taken mercy on him and killed him. They left the weapon beside the body on a Xihji holy book.

Assuming the power surges were from a matter transport device, the Izar did this in thirty-one minutes. The Izar would just obliterate the asteroid rather than come personally, unless Yuud either had or knew something they wanted. Judging from the deli-sliced Xihji before me, if he knew it or had it, they got it.

The remaining Xihji here must be taking everything of value before they abandon this station.

Exiting noiselessly, I moved to one of the computers. I tapped a switch on my battle computer and my virtual interface entered translation mode. As in most remote facilities, they had no security protocol on their systems. I dumped their core backup onto a memory crystal and then made my way back to the Phantom.

"Computer: Analyze Izar ship departure trajectory and plot pursuit course," I said.

A chirp sounded an image appeared on the main display. Something about that picture looked familiar.

"Computer:" I said, "Overlay this image with the course to Iota Centauri!"

The blue line became purple as the two lines overlapped perfectly.

"Engage course, full speed. Forward sensors at maximum. At first sensor contact cut speed to ninety-fuive percent that of contact and sound alert," I ordered.

The same impassionate "Aye, aye" floated across the bridge again.

I had no idea how fast the Izar ship was, but I didn't want to be spotted by them. Fortunately when traveling at hyper velocity you always had a nasty blind spot. To see behind you your scanning wave would have to be travelling at least triple your speed to return with any useful information. The pursuing ship however, could detect star field distortions if they already knew where to look.

A nagging feeling was telling me that the Izars and I were after the same person.

I inserted Yuud's memory dump into a port on the computer console and began to scan the contents. Fortune was smiling that day. The records were current when I copied them. There was no video, but there were audio recordings of his office. The educated guess would be he did a lot of things he didn't want on video.

The screen flashed as I went straight to the end of the latest file and backed up to approximately when the Izars arrived.

"Jwrhlefg soeihgp geh lwiho kjhp," the sound began. I applied the translation filter and the sound suddenly changed. "tr gdjhg the hells do you mean they not responding?"

There was an indistinguishable reply on the poor recording.

"Here? Oh holy Gods of Narod protect Yuud!" he almost screamed.

The sound of footsteps preceded a new voice. A harsh, almost electronic pulsing of tones can over the recording. The translator paused the recording for a couple of seconds then indicated Izari.

"Xihji Yuud Masar! You are guilty of trafficking in stolen Izari technology," the translation said.

Yuud's voice trembled with terror, "No! Please, Izari Yuud's old and dear friend! Yuud did

187

not know was stolen! Strange trader said was brother's invention!

"NO! Unhand Yuud! No, please! Yuud tell truth!" he screamed over the sounds of a struggle.

The Izari voice spoke, "Do you have more of our property?"

"No! Yuud no have!"

A brief hissing sound was drowned out by a scream.

"Do you have more of our property?" the voice asked again.

"Yes! Yuud have one vial Yuud forget!" he screamed.

The Izari voice continued, "Where is it?"

"Yuud will show you… cannot say," he gasped.

The hiss was again lost in the blood-curdling scream. This continued through dozens more questions. Eventually it became answer or not, truth or not, he lost more of his body. He told them that their item was in his wall safe, which the sounds said they cut open with the same savage efficiency.

Yuud was scum, but no one deserved what he went through. I doubt he held anything back from them. I would have certainly been found out if they had known the right questions to ask.

My main advantage at this point was the fact that I knew about them, but they didn't know about me.

If my suspicion was correct and the vial in question was nanobots that would mean that either someone slipped them into Mars base and convinced everyone they built them, or Anna had known all along that they were stolen from the Izari.

It was hard to convince myself that Anna Stotfold was a conspirator in this, even though that was the more probable of the two scenarios.

Unfortunately, no one on the recording said what the property was.

The recording ended about five minutes after the Izari left, when one of Yuud Masar's own people responded to his pleas for death. After that, only the hum of the bad recording could be heard.

I vowed to myself that I would never become a prisoner of the Izari.

This trip was going to take about two weeks at the Phantom's maximum speed, unless I overtook the Izari ship. If their drive technology was as advanced as their weaponry then I stood little chance of catching them.

I looked at my course on the chart. From the perspective of Earth, the Phantom would traverse the entire constellation. The space dogs called it crossing the Centaur.

XVII

Chasing the Truth

The next two weeks were spent analyzing the data acquired so far.

The spectrogram of the Izari ship had revealed that they were indeed much faster than the Phantom. They would beat me there by a good week.

I feared that the Prdynon thief, Wenvin Wo, would meet the same fate as Yuud Masar if the Izari found him first.

They would have to find him in The Thieves Market, and that would require a much more subtle approach than they had used at the remote outpost.

Most people in Wo's line of work didn't advertise, but they frequently had front companies with shops in the bazaar. Wo would be instinctively looking out for anyone he had stolen from, all while looking for the next sale.

On the fourth day sensors picked up a probe near the Phantom's flight path. Its construction was similar to the Izari ship.

The ship went dark as I dropped out of gravity drive and drifted silently toward the alien machine. It was giving off no detectable signals. I risked an active scan while still out of explosion range. Data crept across the display as various bands of radiation penetrated the Izari device. Still no signals.

It appeared to be a beacon of some type, minus a transmitter. No explosives or radiation was detected. A lot could be learned from an up-close inspection of this device. No transmission could overtake the Izari ship at their speed, so it was worth the risk.

When the Phantom was holding within a few meters of the probe, I donned a spacesuit and went out to take a look. Special Services training said that when your quarry does something unexpected, find out why.

Everything that happens is a consequence of another action. Randomness is merely what we don't understand. "Every rock in the universe is where it is because a particular star blew up in a particular way at a particular time!" my Statistical Behavior Prediction instructor used to say. Thus far in my life, I have seen his assertion proven without exception.

Had the Phantom not been intensely scanning the space ahead for the Izari ship, it would not have detected the tiny, stationary probe. It didn't have a propulsion system, but there was a passive sensor array.

The device was less than a meter long, and cylindrical with conical ends. I moved over the surface of it with a molecular scanner, recording details down to its atomic structure. The data was already being processed by the computer back on board.

Preliminary results began to flash in front of me via my virtual interface implant. Standard sensor array. No significant storage on board. No transmitter.

"Computer: If there is no transmitter or storage, where is the data flow directed?" I asked into my helmet mic.

A section of the inner workings of the probe highlighted in front of me, rotated, and expanded. "To a micro sensor array," the computer said.

I tried to imagine what possible use a micro sensor array could be on a deep space probe.

"Computer: What is the micro-array configured to detect?"

The computer replied, "Quantum signals of subatomic particles."

Realization began to dawn. I needed one more answer, "Computer: Is there a tool for manipulating the quantum state?"

"Unknown," came the quick reply, "sixty-eight percent of that module is unknown to my database."

If the data flow was directed to that array, there was little doubt that was a quantum communication device. Earth militaries had attempted to communicate using the odd phenomenon of quantum entanglement, but it was eventually deemed impossible by our best scientists. I guess the Izari had better scientists.

"Computer: What are the external sensors calibrated to look for?" I questioned.

There was a pause and a list appeared. Everything was geared specifically for detecting faster-than-light travel in its range. However, it was designed to detect being scanned, and being moved.

I needed to move quickly. By now, the Izari knew that someone had found their probe. Disabling and deceiving satellites and probes was old territory for me.

Returning quickly to the ship, I offloaded a large metal cargo crate. With the crate tethered to the ship's grapple at such an angle that its sensors were focused on the plain opposite my travel. I maneuvered the probe inside and closed the cover.

Back inside the Phantom, I nudged the controls and headed out on conventional engines in a slow acceleration, off perpendicular to the Izari.

Once we were up to the approximate speed of a long haul freighter, the grapple released and the probe and I parted ways.

I hoped that would convince the Izari that a junk merchant had picked it up as a derelict. The container was radiation shielded so it should fog the readings of the probe's sensors much like a cargo ship's hold.

Breathing a hopeful sigh of relief, I queried the computer once more, "Computer: Calculate approximate Izari ship location based on constant speed and heading. Calculate for the exact time of first active scan of the probe."

A point illuminated in the star field ahead on the 3D display.

"Time to intercept?"

"Eighty-one hours, ten minutes, and twelve seconds travel time at maximum velocity," the dispassionate voice replied.

Reaching out with my finger, I touched the course line and dragged it into an exaggerated 'S' shape centered on where I would have dropped the next probe if I were the Izari commander.

"Time to destination via new course?"   I inquired.

The computer responded instantly, "Eighty-seven hours, two minutes, and forty-three seconds to designated coordinates."

"Implement course at maximum speed. Continue full forward sensor scans, if a target is detected make no change or targeted scan.   Just sound alert," I ordered.

If there was another probe where I predicted that would confirm that the Izari had quantum communication technology, bringing a hidden advantage to light.

With a few days to kill, I began working to convert the ship's small gym into something more suited to my needs.

The nanos were taking care of the fitness of my muscles quite well, but they couldn't help with the reflexes and training. The military had experimented with downloading training directly into the mind, it was quickly realized that this was no substitute for the boring repetitiveness of combat training. Merely knowing which moves to make turned out to be much different from actually making them.

The Phantom's gym only about twice the size of a crew cabin, and was mostly dedicated to cardio training. I removed the few bolts securing the machines to the deck and lowered the ship's gravity. A short time later, they were all secured against a bulkhead in the cargo hold.

Over the next couple of days padding was laid, a heavy bag installed, and a trio of rotating training trees.

The trees were particularly useful. Each one could deliver a padded blow to any part of the body. The trainee (or test dummy, as first timers were called) stands in the middle of the three trees. Each tree has strong but flexible arms protruding horizontally at regular intervals. These arms can inflict painful blows despite being well padded. A computer controls the rotation of each tree, both in speed and direction.

The result is as close to a three against one street fight as you can get. The selectable levels increase the computer's analysis of your style and moves resulting in a bruising defeat even for experts eventually.

Special services training kept you fighting these things throughout your career. A week of intense training preceded every covert mission. From shortly after Earth made first contact with an alien species, varying gravity intensities had been incorporated into the training.

That added a whole new dimension to combat. Injury rates rose higher in training than in the field. The lower the gravity the worse our troops performed. The eventual solution involved tripling the length of basic training, with three months traditional, and six months living and training in zero gravity. Once zero g performance was acceptable, then the other gravity intensities were learned more readily.

I had just emerged from an early morning zero g training session when the sensors alerted to a contact.

Moments later, I was on the bridge studying the object detected. It's mass and makeup matched perfectly. This course passed within about a half million kilometers of the probe, well within its range. Just where I had hoped.

The Phantom's track continued across the probe's view heading away from the Izars course. When well clear of the probe I turned the ship.

"Computer: Resume course to Iota, but plot Y and Z axis offset by one million kilometers," I said hoping to avoid encountering another of the probes.

"Course ready," came the reply.

"Engage at full speed," I said as I left the bridge to find some breakfast.

The next couple of days I spent in the gym on a self-imposed refresher course. The nanobots had been working on my body since they were injected back on Mars. I knew that I had never been fitter, but the extent of their enhancements was quite a surprise.

After working on the combat tree down to zero g, I decided to try something that was considered nearly impossible.

It was time to try fighting the tree in high gravity. The computer wasn't hampered by higher gravity like the combatant is, making it very difficult to avoid the low hits.

At two g, the record was three minutes at level one. In normal gravity, a Special Services agent must qualify at level ten. The higher gravity affected every move you made. Every limb was heaver, you fell faster and harder. The manual recommended that hand-to-hand combat on a high gravity planet be avoided.

I was stunned to discover that I could go to four g before my performance scores began to drop. It made me wonder how far these nanobots would go in 'enhancing' me. I knew that alterations to the brain could change ones very nature, and I didn't even have a way to tell if I was being affected.

201

A quick look through the ships database discovered a few psychological tests that I could use to make a frame of reference before I changed any further.

They had been installed for the shakedown crew of the Phantom to test for cumulative stress patterns from shipboard life. This allowed the design engineers a chance to remove the nuisance problem points that only make a tough job more stressful.

I hoped that over time they would tell me if I was becoming a monster.

When the Phantom arrived at Iota Centauri Four, it was night at The Thieves Market.

The natives call the planet Quinzea. The Quinzean day was just over one hundred and thirty-seven hours long. The natives had evolved with the same cycle, and slept over fifty hours per day.

The Thieves Market, however, never slept.

There were hundreds of ships in the viewer, but the computer highlighted only one in red. It was the Izar ship. It was docked at one of the hundreds of airlocks connected to their space elevator. I pulled the Phantom into a dock on the next pod over where I had a good view of their ship.

"Computer: Monitor the Izar ship. Alert me if it moves," I ordered.

"Aye, aye!" the automated voice confirmed.

The fact that they were still there was encouraging. If they had found Wenvin Wo, they would waste no time in extracting what they wanted from him… one slice at a time.

The flip side of the coin was that if the Izari had been spotted by Wo, he was probably so deep in hiding that no one would find him.

Hitting the streets asking everyone about a stolen Izar technology vendor was guaranteed to end badly. The Izari knew what I knew as far as Wo's whereabouts, therefore, I had to assume that they had already been to his shop and could still be keeping the place under surveillance.

I donned my stealth suit under some more traditional clothes. The plasma sidearm felt right in its customary place under my left arm. My antique

Walther PPK slug thrower was nestled in its own holster in the small of my back. The stealth suit, in addition to being almost invisible at night, was well equipped in the weapons department with a number of close proximity bladed weapons.

There's never a problem with personal weapons in the Frontier Free Trade Zones as they were called. The problems didn't ensue until you killed someone. Then you had better be able to vanish, have proof you were defending yourself, or plenty of money if you wanted to avoid a murder charge.

The currency of choice on the Frontier is holbingite ore certificates. The miners financed their operations by preselling the ore that they were mining. The holbingite was essential for the alloy used in ships hulls. A small percentage in any hull alloy was an effective barrier against cosmic radiation. This made it a highly sought after trading commodity. I still didn't know how I was going to solve the inevitable need for funding.

The money was all that the Quinzeans were interested in. The Thieves Market was on an island continent that straddled the equator. This made it an ideal location for a free trade zone. With the market isolated from the rest of the planet the Quinzeans taxed the trade, held exclusive planet to orbit cargo-shipping rights, and owned the space elevator, while keeping their planet to themselves.

I exited the Phantom and headed down the corridor toward the ticket kiosk for the elevator to the planet, peeling off two bills of my very limited supply of currency.

Man had discovered early on that most planets frowned on alien ships actually landing on the surface due to the risk of ecological contamination. The space elevator let them control planetary access and scan for invasive flora and faunae. Many also had sterilization fields, which killed all surface microorganisms as visitors passed through it.

This one did not. It appeared that every expense had been spared in this barren, utilitarian station.

There were hundreds of different species congregating in the various bars, awaiting the arrival of the next elevator car. Humanoid species are common in the galaxy with various specialized adaptations based on the environment of their particular home worlds.

Reptilians, insectoids, amphibians, and others without an Earthly comparison were also represented in the galaxy. There was even a race that looked suspiciously like the "Grey" aliens who had been in all of the alien encounter stories from old Earth. They were called the D'gotari, and they vehemently denied ever visiting Earth.

The ancient races were rarely seen on the Frontier, and it was rumored that one or more of the ancient races were pure energy life forms. I was certainly interested in meeting one of them, given the chance.

Wenvin Wo was an insectoid about a meter and a half tall, and walked as a quadruped. He had compound eyes and his two arms reminded me of Earth's praying mantis.

I stopped and stared at Wo's picture on my virtual display. I had seen this somewhere recently.

Quickly backtracking toward the Phantom I came across a digital billboard displaying wanted fugitives believed to be hiding somewhere in the market. There was an insectoid on the display who was definitely Wo's species, if not Wo himself. Having never met a Prdynon I didn't know enough about them to distinguish Wenvin Wo from any other Prdynon.

At the first touch, the image enlarged and displayed the particulars of this unfortunate creature. The translation appeared in my vision. It was Wo.

He was charged with piracy. One thing stood out. The bounty for him was enough to buy your own freighter, but alive only. Bounties were usually put up by the shipper who had been attacked, and they rarely wanted to waste their time with a trial for the offender. Moreover, they felt it sent a message to other pirates to leave them alone. 'Alive only' was unusual to say the least.

That meant the Izari hadn't found him yet. Either they went down and he bolted before they caught him, or they had decided to let scum search for scum with a hefty reward paid through blind channels.

I had no doubt that a number of bounty hunters were already on his trail considering the price.

XVIII

The Quinzea Spacelift

A klaxon sounded indicating the arrival of an elevator car. Suddenly the hundreds of different beings moved as one, pouring out of the bars, cafes, and waiting areas and heading for the central core of the station.

The corridor leading to the boarding level was an eye twisting sight. It corkscrewed one hundred and eighty degrees, turning everyone upside down as they walked. The gravity plating made it feel like you were walking on level ground, giving the eerie impression that you were turning the station beneath you.

On the boarding level, the elevator was just arriving. It rose silently, clinging to a jet-black, ten-meter thick tether that was anchored deep inside the asteroid as a counterweight for the space elevator. The other end was anchored on Quinzea, about tow hundred and thirty-eight thousand kilometers away. Because of the planet's slow rotation, it was a long ride from this high geostationary orbit.

I wondered how crowded it would be on the way down with this many um... people, waiting to get on. The IP database had only said there were two cars in constant motion to and from the planet.

Approaching the transparent doors, I glimpsed the building arching away in the distance at least a kilometer away. My view was suddenly cut off by the arrival of the elevator car, if you could call it that. It fully filled the one-kilometer void in the middle of the station. Finally, as the whole thing appeared I could tell that the car was built in a huge spiral shape.

When the car was sealed fast to the station the transparent doors on both the station and the car lowered noisily into the floor. Throngs of creatures began to pour off in every direction. Some pushed levitation carts loaded with cases, and some appeared to be on vacation. These seedy places always draw a certain type who have a taste for taboo and come for hedonistic purposes only.

After the bulk of the new arrivals had disembarked, I stepped on board and began to make my way to the end of the car. As long as I was there I might as well learn something, I thought. Downtime in foreign territory was reconnaissance time. An old and faded informational sign adorned a wall outside the complex and widely varied toilet facilities, which my battle computer translated as:

"The Quinzea Spacelift
Commission #276957299
Kree Shipworks
Gamma Centauri

This ultimate example of modern
orbital transit technology was
built to specification by the
master designers and craftsmen
at the famous Kree Shipworks.
The asteroid was specially

selected for mass, density, shape, and placed in orbit under contract with Botreiki Mining. The tether you see through the center window was manufactured on the asteroid and lowered to the planet. It is comprised of quadrillions of intricately woven nanotubes woven into a low mass tether that's over ten meters across. With safety and huge capacity in mind, engineers designed in a tenfold safety margin. It would take a mass ten times that of the anchor asteroid to even begin to stress the tether..."

It went on to describe how it employed a spiral design that allowed the two cars to pass each other on the same cable by slowing and rotating in opposite directions to pass each other as smoothly as a nut passing over a bolt. It recommended locations for photo opportunities and mentioned the time into the trip that the spiral passing occurred.

I could just imagine some politician touting the benefits of this massive project to the Quinzeans, and couldn't resist chuckling to myself.

A series of oscillating noises reminiscent of neighing soprano horse sounded beside me. The translator paused as it identified the language then subtitles appeared in my vision just beneath the being emitting the sound.

"Grandiose description of a worn-out pile of scrap metal, isn't it my friend?" he laughed.

"Junk to some, miraculous sorcery to others!" I said, as I looked him over. He/she/neither/both appeared to be a combination of mammal and reptile, and about half my height, but double my width. Long muscular arms emerged from beneath its shiny black fur. A broad head held side-facing eyes near the top protected by a scaled ridge. Its face was furred down to its reptilian looking mouth.

The almost equine laugh again emerged from the creature. "You make a good point! Forgive my forwardness. I do not know your world or its customs, and I am a very curious man! May we make each other's journey pass quickly with the pleasure of conversation?" he asked.

"It would be my pleasure. It has been a long time since I have had a conversation purely for pleasure! My name is Mac," I said with a smile.

A high sound came from him that didn't translate and his eyes brightened as he replied, "I am called Lobruc. Let us find a place to have a drink!" he said as one of his eyes scanned the area, "You come from carbon as well, do you like alcohol?"

Guessing he meant I was a carbon based life form I replied, "Yes, I come from carbon. Alcohol sounds fine. Lead on, Lobruc."

A short while later we pushed through a crowded cantina and found a table with seats suitable to our anatomy. "I must apologize for how I sound," Lobruc said, "the thin air of this station affects my voice and makes me sound like a bird."

I glanced at my battle computer readout out of curiosity. The air pressure here was about twenty percent above Earth normal. He had to be from a planet with a very thick atmosphere. Guessing from his fur, it was cold as well. "Is your world far away, Lobruc?" I asked.

"My home is called Sooggao Uxi. It is a very beautiful world just over one hundred light years toward the galactic center. The most beautiful colors fill the night sky as the sun reflects off of the rings. I miss it very much. What world is your home, Mac?"

Training overrode amiability and I lied, "I come from the planet Volkswagen. It's located about two hundred light years away toward the Ford galaxy." I wasn't about to give anyone a map back to Earth. The planet would be ripe for invasion for a long time with no defenses. The fewer people who knew, the better.

"I do not know of these places," he said.

I smiled, imagining his confusion if the names I used had been in the translator's database. I knew that no proper names were listed, and the two extinct companies wouldn't mind anymore.

"Yes, we are in the middle of nowhere. I have not been there in a very long time. Space travel is socially frowned upon there, and aliens are unwelcome. A bit xenophobic really. I guess that is why I never go back," I said.

Lobruc nodded, "These days I can see the lure of withdrawing from the decadence of the galaxy, but for we men of adventure no planet has gravity strong enough to hold us down! What is your profession, Mac?"

"I sell farming technology," I said, using one of the Special Service identities that I had used before.

"Ah! A lucrative trade on every world! Everyone has to eat, and carnivore or herbivore, all food starts with the soil," he mused.

Lobruc seemed to be a very outgoing sort of person. Not what one would expect to run into by chance on the way to a black market bazaar. The hairs on the back of my neck were standing on end the same way they had the last time I had been made as an undercover agent. I was definitely a subject of interest to him, but why?

"What do you do, Lobruc?" I inquired, "Not a farm owner by chance?"

The horselaugh echoed again, "No, I'm no potential sale I'm afraid! However, you might be a client for me... I own a freighter. I come here as there are always jobs. The more exciting, the more pay. It is a win, win situation!"

"If you ignore the third variable," I said.

"What is the third variable?"

"Danger. It always stays near its brothers."

He nodded, "Without the danger you would have no excitement!"

"It can become an addiction for some," I observed.

Lobruc may have had a taste for adventure, but I wasn't buying his story. His large hands had wear signs the same as any human would. Anyone handling cargo and running a ship will develop wear patterns on the underside of their hands from the manual labor. The upper classes would have very little change, and the fighters have the damage to

217

the backs and sides of their hands. Lobruc was the latter.

"Of all my addictions, I like danger most. It reminds me I am alive. I am affecting the universe," he said.

"That's remarkable indeed," I said, "for a freighter captain."

One of Lobruc's eyes was always in motion. First one would look at me and the other patrolled the room, then they switched.   It was very disconcerting.   In their position, it would be nearly impossible to approach him undetected.

"Mac, let us drop the pretense," he said as he leaned in. "I know why you are here and you know why I am here. It is a big reward and plenty for both of us."

My mind raced. He was a bounty hunter and thought I was as well. That came as a relief. The Izari might still be clueless to my existence.

"I'm thinking the reward wouldn't be that large unless this is one tough bastard," I said.

"How do I know you wouldn't try to kill me and take all the reward after we capture him?"

Lobruc seemed taken aback. "I don't have to be a criminal to be a bounty hunter. It is still an honest profession, despite the thugs who usurp the name."

I rubbed my chin, "I will do it on one condition. I want an hour alone with Wo before we collect."

"But the reward is alive only my friend, and I'm afraid I can't sanction torture," he protested.

"I don't intend to harm him. I just need some answers. How do you know torture doesn't await him when you turn him in?" I probed.

"I must have faith in the authorities following the Free Trade Zone Pact. What happens to him in their hands I cannot control, but I must live with what happens to anyone in my custody," he said with both eyes focused on me.

"Lobruc, if you are telling the truth, we will get along fine. If you are lying to me, I will kill you," I said meeting his gaze coldly.

He stood to his full height and his left arm crossed his chest, "If I were to do such a dishonorable thing, my death would be a favor to the shattered souls of my ancestors."

I lowered my head in respect for his display, and he sat back down. "There is a Prdynon sector here where Wenvin Wo would likely have friends and family," I began.

"This everyone knows. The Zone Guards have searched all known associates' homes and businesses. This I get from a Zone Guard Captain for whom I have found fugitives before," Lobruc said.

"I had figured that. I have never met Wo before personally, but he has a reputation of being highly intelligent and resourceful. He isn't in the Prdynon sector. He has to have shady contacts from other worlds."

"I agree. But most of the disreputable types would turn in their own den mother for a reward this large."

I nodded, "Exactly. That will help us narrow down where he might be!"

"It is unlikely he could afford to beat the reward offer for assistance, not in ready cash anyway, and asset liquidation on that scale makes ripples to be seen," he added with one eye and then the other, still scanning the room.

"Are there any groups who wouldn't value the ore certificates?" I asked.

Lobruc paused, and said, "The only ones I can think of would be miners. They readily spend the certificates as currency, but you will never see them accept one as payment."

"And unknown customers or employers in his shady dealings. His exposure could expose them as well," I added.

Lobruc nodded, "That is a good thought, but wouldn't he see that as an obvious lead? Access to the rest of the planet is tightly controlled and the elevator is monitored. His ship is at his dock, so we know he is on the planet..."

221

"Unless he left his ship as a diversion and departed quietly on another vessel," I cut in.

"That too, is possible."

"Do you know when his ship arrived?"

"It hasn't moved in two Quinzean days."

I did the mental math. That was over eleven Earth days. That would be about right for him coming direct from Yuud Masar's outpost. "And when was the reward posted?" I asked Lobruc.

"One local day ago."

"That means when he arrived here two days ago, he no idea he was in trouble with the Zone Guard, and would therefore have had no reason to bolt," I concluded. "He's in the market. Wenvin Wo is a bug. When threatened I'm willing to be he's going to act like any other cockroach and hide under the nearest piece of furniture."

A puzzled expression crossed Lobruc's face. "Why would he pretend to be genitals under the furniture? Surely the Zone Guard would have found that!"

I couldn't help but laugh at the translations sometimes, "No! A cockroach is a species of insect vermin on my world. It has nothing to do with anything's genitals!"

The brightly colored arch over his eyes shifted from red to orange as my new companion produced what I am going to call his laugh. It reminded me of my childhood and the noises our cat would make at night when he had hairballs.

"I am very sorry for the misinterpretation! It makes me wonder about the rest of our conversations," he said.

"Are you familiar to the locals in the Prdynon district?" I asked.

He shook his head, "I have never been there."

"What about others of your species?" I probed, "I have seen problems with mistaken identities in these places, and the less attention we attract the better."

"There will be no problem."

223

There was a sudden increase in gravity as the car began to slow.

Lobruc stood up and motioned for me to do the same, "The cars are about to pass. It is a very interesting thing if you have never seen it before! I still enjoy it myself!"

"Lead on!" I said as I stood up. I had been looking forward to seeing this event.

The spiral design of the cars allowed the two to pass while riding on the single ten-meter thick cable. It was an interesting feat of engineering. One that I would like to observe from the outside someday.

Lobruc took me down the spiral to an observation section that was completely transparent. "The other end is like this too, for the return trip!" he said excitedly.

It was certainly breathtaking! We were still far above the atmosphere, which Lobruc had explained was essential for the cars to pass properly. Looking down the cable was dizzying even for me. I could see a bulge on the cable coming toward us. I looked up to point it out to Lobruc, and noticed that all the stars were spinning! Or rather, appeared to be spinning. We must be rotating to be up to speed when we get to the Rubicon. The inertia dampeners seemed to be doing their job well. If they failed while we were at speed, it would liquefy everyone on board.

The object approaching was growing at an amazing rate. It looked like a missile headed directly toward our car. There was a sudden flash as the cars intertwined for a few thousandths of a second. It gave the eerie impression that the other car had just passed through us.

"Very exciting indeed!" exclaimed Lobruc.

I was rather startled when I looked around. Every creature with fur or hair was smoothing it down. Lobruc looked very fluffy. With some difficulty, I managed not to laugh.

"There is a huge static effect on both cars when they pass at such speeds," he said. "The observation sections are unshielded for the affect," he concluded as he groomed.

I smiled, "It's quite an effect, Lobruc!   Now let us find a place to sit and formulate our plan for the   surface."

XIX

The Thieves Market

A wall of hot, muggy air hit our faces as we exited the space elevator. I looked up to see a massive transparent geodesic dome enclosing the whole of the island.

"A horrid place is it not?" offered Lobruc.

I agreed with him. "The air is very polluted!" I said as my battle computer listed toxin after toxin in the air samples.

Lobruc pointed up. "That's the reason. The Quinzeans require bio filters on all air transfer points. There are too few of them and they are poorly maintained. They only repair a few them when death rates spike," he said.

We made our way along the crowded streets past shops containing almost anything you could imagine, from drugs to engine parts. Almost two kilometers later the buildings and tents got much shorter and we began to see more Prdynons.

I stopped at one of the plethora of tents and began looking at merchandise on a table.

"Did you find something of interest?" Lobruc asked softly.

"Look at the door directly behind this stall," I said, drawing his attention to a doorway going into a basement shop.

Wenvin Wo

Importer/Exporter
Purveyor of the finest luxury items!

Lobruc covered the street while I walked down the steps and opened the door.

The inside of the shop was cluttered with goods for sale. A few items were recognizable; many were not.

A loud buzzing of wings announced the return of the shopkeeper. The Prdynon didn't seem to have the power of flight, but they used their wings very effectively to convey their mood. The creature before me was about the size of a large dog on Earth. It had a exoskeleton with a metallic glint, like a beetle. It walked on its rear four legs, and used its front two legs as arms.

"What is it you would like today bi-ped? Some dried Yatasao root perhaps? It will make the females want to mate for hours!" the green and gold insect said.

I stood silently for a moment. "Do I have the honor of addressing Mr. Wenvin Wo?" I asked very formally.

The creature made an annoyed clicking sound and rubbed it's antennae in consternation. "I tell everyone already. Mr. Wo is not a pirate, and I don't know where he is," it sputtered.

Remaining expressionless, I said, "Operating on assumptions is the first step toward failure, my diminutive friend. I have no interest in what Mr. Wo does on his own time. I do, however, have an interest in obtaining some hard to find items for a private collector."

Its wings fluttered with delight, "Many apologies! Disregard everything I said! I am Azivdeo. What is the gentleman looking for?"

"He is in the market for a new device built by the Sooggao. They are being very unreasonable at parting with this technology despite a very generous offer. I have it on good authority that Mr. Wenvin Wo is often able to acquire technology through 'creative negotiation'. We would like to contract him to be our purchasing representative," I said maintaining my even demeanor.

The wings buzzed excitedly, "I am sure Mr. Wo will be interested!"

"You speak for Mr. Wo?" I queried.

"I am Wenvin Wo's piunar. I serve and advise him. That is my purpose. I do as Mr. Wo would have me do," the Prdynon said.

I didn't know what a piunar was, but from the context, I guessed it was some type of valet or mentor. "Very well. My employer is not a patient individual. Wealth and power are not conducive to that trait."

I turned my head away and coughed. Concealed in my hand was a tiny dart gun, which fired a tiny dart containing a video camera. An indicator flashed on my virtual display indicating a successful link.

"If Mr. Wo is not available I shall look elsewhere," I said as I turned to leave.

"Wait!" the bug exclaimed, "How can I contact you when Mr. Wo returns?"

I stopped without turning back to him and said, "You can't. I have another individual to interview. I expect he will actually be there for the event, unlike Mr. Wo. If... IF this person is unsatisfactory, I will call here again tomorrow at the same time." The door closed with a bang as I exited the shop.

Lobruc followed me at a distance until we were well outside the Prdynon district, where we met at a café for a drink.

"I know where he is," I told Lobruc after we sat down. "My sensors detected sewer gasses lingering on his clerk, Azivdeo, when he came out

231

of the back room. Also, can you think of a place less likely to be searched than the sewer on a hot, humid planet? The gasses alone would kill most life forms, but not most insectoids."

"I can go into the sewers with a breather," offered Lobruc.

"Hopefully it won't come to that. There's kilometers of tunnels down there, and Wo can squeeze through holes neither of us could fit through. It will be better to let him come to us. I left a bit of cheese with his clerk. Hopefully that will draw him out," I said, sipping my drink.

"What is this 'cheese' you speak of? Is it a tracking device?" asked Lobruc.

I laughed, "No! Cheese is the bait they use on my world to lure rodent vermin into a trap. Lobruc, you may not know it, but you have a very valuable piece of technology on your ship! Wenvin Wo is going to be hired to steal it."

"I am liking this idea! How will he get to the station, do you think?" he asked.

"I'm sure he has his resources, but if he can't manage it on his own, we will offer to help him out," I said, "Either way, we have him."

"When do you meet the clerk again?" he inquired.

"Tomorrow. Same time."

Lobruc cocked his head in surprise, "That is a very long time on this planet. What if someone else claims our prize in the meantime?"

I shook my head, "I doubt it. Those tunnels are a maze. Wo knows them. So even if someone thought of going there the odds would still be heavy in Wenvin Wo's favor. The other reason for the delay is to give Wo time to think about it long enough to get greedy. The type of job I offered is very lucrative by its nature. He will want the funding boost to help him deal with this piracy charge, whether by legal means or relocating and restarting, the money could be a game changer."

I slid a small device across the table to Lobruc. "I will contact you on this," I said, "We need to go our separate ways until the meeting time. Me being seen with the person I want robbed could be disastrous. I'm going to get a room at the Spacelift Hotel, and play the shady tech buyer for whoever might be watching."

"So what is this unusual technology that I harbor on my ship?" Lobruc asked.

I smiled, "A '57 Chevy," I said thinking that there was no way that would translate to anything meaningful. "It was a primitive form of transport on my home world. It was so poorly designed that it used exploding gasoline to propel. Now, however, it's valuable breakthrough technology from Sooggao Uxi!"

Lobruc's eyes came together on me for a rare moment, and he said, "I will assume the role of business traveler then. I will take a room at the hotel as well and await your signal."

With that, we parted ways. I checked in at the hotel, grateful for the air conditioning. After inspecting the room and scanning for recording/transmitting devices, I went to the hotel bar to be visible. I was certain that Wo would have someone check up on me. The next seventy hours of my life were spent between my room and the hotel bars. I occasionally saw Lobruc out of the corner of my eye. At no point did he show any sign of recognition. He was good, whether by training or birth. I found myself hoping that he was as good as his word. He could be a useful ally.

*****

Before the next day dawned, I had secreted myself on the roof of Wenvin Wo's building.

A few taps on my battle computer and the micro video camera I had fired into a dark corner of Wo's shop the previous day uploaded it's file to me. These cameras record video and sound for up to a month before a download was necessary. It was shielded so that no detector could detect its energy signature. The only weakness was the millisecond time when it uploaded the video.

From my concealed location, I reviewed the video on my virtual interface, extracting any segments with noise or motion above ambient levels.

The first thing recorded was my departure.

Azivdeo was complaining aloud to himself shortly after the door had closed. "The young fool never listens. I told him that job would be the end of us. There's a reason no one steals from them. Young fool!" he muttered. He picked up a small statuette and flung it across the room. "Imagine treating his piunar this way. I would be resting now if I had been given a normal hatchling," he said as he pulled a length of pipe from a drawer and inserted it into the drain.

His high-pitched chirping voice carried through the plumbing to the sewers.

This method was as simplistic as it was genius. No electronic communication to be intercepted, no couriers to be trusted. Moreover, from his position in the sewers he had literally thousands of tunnels to hide in if a direct attack were to come in through the shop above.

"Wo? Are you still there, boy?" he asked into the tube.

The recorder didn't pick up the response, but Azivdeo heard one.

"It's a client. A profitable client if you will come out of the drain and get back to work!" he said.

Another pause then he said, "There have been no zigs here in three days... How am I supposed to know? I can't leave the shop unattended to go anywhere to find out anything," he chirped.

"The creature may be back tomorrow if we are lucky. If you pass up this job, I will recommend to the queen that our hive assets be reassigned when I die. I am old and tired and can't keep going...," he snapped into the hose before throwing it roughly aside.

So... Wenvin Wo was, at least to his piunar, just a headstrong larva who had pissed off some bad people, and was now afraid to come out of the sewers. If the Zone Guard had recruited a few Prdynons they would have had him quickly, but the Quinzeans were far too large in stature to pursue an insectoid in confined spaces.

I continued to scan the video clips, finding nothing more interesting than random customers

237

buying, selling, trading and most of all haggling, which Azivdeo engaged with obvious glee. That was until a few hours after dark.

The monochromatic image of infrared was triggered once again by motion. At the base of a large display case in the center of the main floor a board under the edge fell forward. An insectoid arm pushed the board back from the opening and a flattened form emerged from the six-inch opening.

There must me a floor drain or purpose built escape hatch under the heavy case. If the Zone Guard did find this they would probably have looked under it and discounted it as nothing more than a broken pedestal.

The form stood up to its full height, stretched, and went to a cupboard. He was just opening the door when I heard the old bug's voice ring out from the back. Wo jumped at the sound.

"Wo, is that you?" Azivdeo chirped as he pointed a bright light at the younger Prdynon. Wenvin Wo's exoskeleton glistened like a multicolored jewel under the intense light. I saved a still of the image for reference.

"Shit Azi! You frightened me! Turn that light off before the zigs see it!" Wo chirped softly.

"Here you come sneaking back in the middle of the night like a common thug!" Azivdeo admonished. "Wait until the queen hears about this! We will lose everything!"

Wo put his arm around the old insect and spoke in a reassuring voice, "Piunar, I will never leave you to the birds. I am back to get the job. If this is as good as you say then we will have enough money to relocate where the damned Izari can never find us!"

"Do you mean it, boy? Are you going to get serious about the business?" Azivdeo questioned.

"I was wrong. I didn't think they would ever notice they were missing, much less be able to figure out who took them. Forgive me piunar," Wo implored.

"Good!" Azivdeo said with a sudden sharpness in his tone, "Now, if you do as you're told we can get off this rock before the Izari can dissect us. When the biped comes back…"

Wo made a gesture, "What if they already gave the job..."

"Don't you think I thought of that!" Azivdeo cut in. "The instant he left here I sent a message that there was an alien here trying to track someone stealing supplies from official Quinzean cargo shipments," he held up a hand to stop Wo before he spoke. "Yes, I know everyone does that, and that's precisely why no one in this gods forsaken dome will talk to a hairless mammal biped. They are all guilty."

"So he will have to come back to us," Wo concluded.

I began to wonder how Wo had managed to steal anything from the Izari. He didn't seem like the smartest egg in the sac. An opinion shared by his own family it appeared.

The old Prdynon continued, "So he will have to come to us. Then you will agree to the job, providing he makes arrangements to get us both off the planet. Have you got that?"

"Yes, Piunar," Wo said with resignation in his movements.

The exchange ended shortly thereafter with Wo returning to the small space near the floor drain for the night, and Azivdeo returned to the small cubbyhole overlooking the shop that seemed to be his sleeping area.

Nothing significant happened on through the night until the first customer banged on the door, then it was routine business. I was about to the end of the recorded video when something caught my eye.

Another Prdynon had entered from the street and walked directly to Azivdeo. The two touched antennae in a rapid tapping motion. Azivdeo lowered his head to the stranger, who then exited saying nothing.

Something about this made me very uneasy. Lobruc was already on his way back to his ship to set an automatic containment field, so I was on my own once again.

With a sigh, I secured my gear and headed for a café to pass the time until my appointment.

XX

Murphy's Law is Universal

At the appointed time, I opened the door to Wenvin Wo's shop and walked inside, with my battle computer silently scanning for any threats.

A buzzing of wings preceded the chirps of Azivdeo, "Can I help... oh! It's you. I guess your other prospect didn't pan out?"

"He too was unreachable. Have you corrected your communications fault or have I wasted my time?" I asked with a steady gaze.

"I apologize for not greeting you personally yesterday," said a voice emerging from behind the large display case. "Wenvin Wo, eager to be of assistance... to those who can afford my services."

"There is nothing my employer desires that he cannot afford." I looked him over critically, "You... are the acquisition specialist? I fear your reputation may have been exaggerated. You

243

appear too fragile for this type of work. My employer will not tolerate a failed attempt. He would be very angry with me for selecting you, and I, in turn, would be very... very... unkind to you."

Wo stood taller and light danced across his colorful body. "I am the best thief on this planet," he chirped, "and..."

It was at this point a force known as Murphy's Law chose to remind me that it was, in fact, a universal law. For at that moment, everything that could go wrong, went wrong.

Before Wo could finish his sentence, the entrance door was propelled into the room by an explosion. An instant later Zone Guards poured in with weapons drawn. Wo turned to retreat to his escape route only to be face to face with a Guard rifle. He raised his hands in surrender.

I had no choice but to join him.

"Wenvin Wo, you slippery bastard!" roared the leader of the group, "They were going to make me go into that damned sewer after you! I just wanted to gas you but no. They must have you alive."

The rather large Quinzean walked over to Azivdeo, who was the only one of us without guns pointed at him. He pulled out a stack of notes and handed them to the old insect, who clutched them gleefully.

"Piunar! You turned me in? How could you do that?" Wenvin Wo screeched.

Azivdeo walked over to be face to face with the restrained Wo, "You never listened to me, the one charged with making you a productive member of our fractured hive. You were always trying to be flashy and get noticed. That is not the way of the Prdynon," The old bug hissed. "Now you have the audacity to steal from them and bring pressure down on our whole community.

"The queen decided. You are expelled from the hive, making it perfectly acceptable for me to collect my retirement by selling you since I couldn't by training you! I hope they boil you in your own shell!" he spat as Azivdeo turned and scuttled away.

He paused at the doorway and said over his shoulder, "Oh and if you are crafty enough to get out of this, I don't recommend ever coming back among your people. There's a Royal Death Warrant being issued as we speak. Goodbye you ungrateful boy!"

While everyone was transfixed on the unfolding family drama, I hit the transmit button on my link to Lobruc and placed it among the trinkets on the counter.

The Zone Guard Commander walked over and peered down at me. "What," he asked, "are you?"

"Merely an art dealer looking for a bargain, Commander," I told him, "I can see there will be no further sales here today, so I will leave you gentlemen to your business!"

A guttural sound emanated from his bluish bulk. "Bring him too," he grunted.

Another burley Guard shuffled up and clamped paralysis cuffs both my arms just above the elbow, then we were led out of the building to a waiting vehicle. I knew it would be foolish to escape here, as the only way off the planet from here was the elevator. It would be better to simply let them take where I wanted to go.

We were roughly shoved inside the Guard van, and the heavy door slammed shut and we began to pick our way through the narrow streets to the elevator.

"Wenvin Wo, I am not who I said I was," I began, "I am, however, in a unique position to get you out of here when I leave."

"Who are you? And how do you propose we get out of here and off the planet?" he demanded.

"My name is unimportant. We won't know each other that long, no matter whether you choose to live or die. Now, if you do as you are told and answer my questions, I swear I will deliver you alive to your ship. After that you're on your own." I said in an urgent whisper.

I was getting data from my battle computer about the van. It was bugged, however the poorly insulated vehicle combined with horrid roads produced ample road noise to obscure a soft conversation.

Wo relented, "What choice do I have?"

I shook my head grimly, "After seeing was left of Yuud Masar when the Izari left, you really don't."

My developing enhanced vision showed a change in Wo's temperature patterns, as fear gripped him.

"I will tell you anything you want to know," he said with his antennae drooping.

"What was it you stole from Izar?"

"It was a very tiny drop of silver liquid; I'm telling you it was smaller than a grain of sand."

"Who did you steal it for?" I questioned.

His antennae rose again, "It was a creature like you! I knew you looked familiar when I first saw you in the shop! Yuud Masar had arranged the meeting. They told me that it was a new medicine that the Izari would not share, and that thousands would die without it!"

That sounded farfetched, to anyone who hadn't been inside Special Services. Lying or not in this case, they had done that, and worse before.

"So you have no idea what it was you took?" I asked.

"If it wasn't medicine, then no!" he answered quickly.

I tried a new direction, "Who was your human contact?"

"His name was Black Bird."

Something jolted in my memory. There was black ops agent that they called the Raven. I checked the translator and confirmed that Raven and Black Bird were exactly the same in Wo's language. I reset the translation value to match.

That meant that the manhunt and dramatic capture was just a show to cover his new employment at IP Industries. The picture of what had brought about the terrible destruction of Earth was becoming clearer.

"How are you going to get us out of here?" Wo asked.

"Just be ready to move when I tell you. Why escape now, when they are taking us right to our ships?" I replied.

"Those cells on the station are carved out in the nickel-iron of the asteroid itself, secured with a laser grid door. There is no way out of them," he said sadly.

"Trust me," I said as I wondered myself.

A short time later, the van arrived at the Spacelift. They had timed their raid to coincide with the car schedule, as they had learned that escapees into the Market disappeared quickly without trace.

We were taken directly to a holding cell in the administrative section of the elevator car. During our brief time in the common area, I spotted the shape of Lobruc sitting at a bar. The figure gave no indication of recognizing me. I hoped he hadn't seen the arrest and decided to cut his losses and run.

I had made it clear to Wenvin Wo that I did not wish to talk.   Most detention facilities were monitored, and idle chatter was a rich source of intelligence.

*****

About halfway into the trip I began to have odd sensations in my arms where there had been nothing since the paralysis cuffs were applied.

Paralysis cuffs were standard in the Frontier. They strapped on, and would work on any form of appendage a creature might sport.   They also allowed the arresting officer to forego dangerous, uncontrolled searches in the field.   In the station all weapons, contraband, or stolen items would be recorded along with complete video documentation of them being removed from the arrestee.

They worked by dampening the neural impulses controlling the limbs, rendering them numb and useless. You could be armed how you like, but unless you could draw and fire your weapon with your teeth, you were pretty much helpless. Without your arms for balance, even foot combat would be ineffectual.

However, something was happening to me. I was regaining sensation. Limited movement was returning to my digits. The nanobots must be shielding the nerves from the dampening field somehow.

Hours later, when we arrived at the station, I had full feeling back in my arms.

XXI

The Escape

The guards came and led us to separate holding cells at the Zone Guard command center. I stepped inside with my arms hanging limply at my sides and sat on the bench directly beneath the security camera.

Leaning forward to conceal the movement I slipped the paralysis cuff off of one arm, then in a flash of sudden movement I slipped the still active cuff around the camera. The glow of its power indicator winked out.

Moving forward slowly I could see no movement in the corridor. If the rumors that no one had ever escaped these cells were true, then security might be a little bit on the lax side.

A few seconds later I could hear alarm sounds drifting down the corridor, the sound of running feet passed nearby then faded into the distance.

I quickly dropped to one knee and pulled a polished silver mirror out of a pocket, and carefully slid it into the path of one of the laser bars. Each cell had twenty emitters pointing down, and twenty pointing across, creating a grid, which would take the failure of at least four lasers to permit an escape. I intercepted the beam and guided it to a small access panel in the ceiling that allowed the power feeds to be serviced, showering the corridor with sparks along the way. When the beam hit the power junction, the resulting blast knocked out the power to the whole section.

Slipping the cuff off my other arm and into a pocket, I quickly removed them from Wo's arms.

"How did you…" he began.

"No time now. Stay close to me!" I yelled, as I moved down the corridor. I knew alarms would draw the station staff back in a hurry. The main corridor in front of the Zone Guard command center was a mass of people running away from the elevator car area I could see Lobruc gesturing from the doorway. Following his gaze, I saw the single

Quinzean Guard manning the communications console.

Silently I circled the desks keeping behind the massive creature. When I was a couple of meters away, I activated the paralysis cuff and pressed the emitter against the back of his head. He slumped to the ground as all neural activity ceased momentarily. He would be all right in a couple of hours save a nasty headache. Wo and I moved quickly towards Lobruc and we all faded into the crowd. Wo fell back and disappeared into the crowd. After a quick shouted conference with Lobruc, we headed for our respective ships.

It appeared everyone else on the station had the same idea.

A few minutes later, the airlock of the Phantom sealed behind me and I released the docking clamps and moved off into the cloud of sudden departures from the station. I didn't know which ship was Wenvin Wo's until I saw the Izar ship turn and follow a group of ships that was heading away from the system.

They were definitely following him. I followed them at a distance trying desperately to think of a way to get Wo out of harm's way. The pursued ship began to make erratic manoeuvers in an attempt to evade the much more advanced Izar ship.

Once again, the familiar energy spike from Yuud Masar's outpost, and then Wo's ship spun out of control faster and faster until centrifugal forces ripped the ship apart.

I had little doubt that the Izari had transported him aboard before the ship spun out of control. A touch of satisfaction was felt as I steered away from the Izar ship and headed to my rendezvous with Lobruc.

*****

The Phantom passed silently through the inky blackness of space. A lone sensor detected a brief glint of reflected starlight. It sent a digital signal to its subprocessor, that signal was evaluated and that subprocessor sent a priority signal to the ships core computer. The computer responded by focusing every sensor it had on the track of the millisecond glint of starlight. Ultraviolet, infrared, electro-magnetic, every bandwidth that the Phantom could monitor fed data back to the core computer.

They all read nothing, but that nothing was moving closer.

All of this happened in less than one second, and culminated with an indicator flashing on my virtual display.

I acknowledged the notification on my battle computer with a smile. "Take THAT Murphy!" I thought aloud as I headed to the ship-to-ship airlock.

Halfway there I received a microburst message from the strange ship. I acknowledged it and sent instructions to the Phantom's computer.

A few moments later, the airlock hissed, and then swung open revealing the luminescent form of Wenvin Wo.

"Did you have any problems?" I asked as he boarded the Phantom.

Wo stroked his antennae, "Your plan worked better than I had hoped! I had just got back to my ship, and before I could send it out on autopilot, another Prdynon I was acquainted with, saw me and begged for a ride. In all of the confusion, he was worried about getting caught with a load of weapons. He had pulled his ship's memory core, released its docking clamps, and was looking for a way off the station. I figured why bother programming the autopilot when I had a volunteer for this particular suicide mission. Did you see what happened to him?" Wo asked.

"Yes, the Izari got him," I confirmed.

Wo fluttered his shiny wings, "Oh well. He was a thorax mite anyway. And, the bastard cheated when we played Wehek!"

I feigned indignation, "The nerve!"

We turned and I led him toward the lounge.

The human chairs weren't suited for Wo's insectoid form, but he seemed to have no problem with just sitting back on his abdomen.

I sat down at the table opposite him. "Do you think they will figure out that wasn't you?" I asked.

Wo shook his head. "Unlikely," he chirped. "We were from the same brood, so we're genetically identical. They would be expecting me to use the 'You've got the wrong bug!' story. They would have to have another member of the Wenvin hive to identify me by smell."

"Searching for someone based on name only is an uphill battle when they don't want to be found," I agreed.

Wo's antennae drooped sadly, "They can't even look for a name now. I am no longer of the hive Wenvin."

I actually felt sympathy for him, as I was in a very similar situation. "Okay Wo, it's time for the rest of your story. I know you didn't just stroll into a lab on Izar and take some nanobots and walk away. Do you have someone on the inside?" I questioned as I tossed him a food pak and opened one for myself. He opened his pak and began to nibble on the nutrient bar.

I was startled when he spoke even though he was still nibbling away on the bar, and then the realization occurred that his chirping was coming from his wings. That would explain why Prdynons still had wings despite apparently being flightless.

"Yes, I owe you my life. You saved me when my own piunar sold me out to the zigs. I will tell you anything you want to know. There was someone on the inside who brought the nanobots to me. He was a scientist with a taste for forbidden pleasures. He was sent to me by the human called Raven. He paid me very well to get the Izari any perverted pleasure he desired. It was easy. He was heavily addicted to hallucinogens, and Raven gave him something new that totally consumed him.

"I got him anything he asked for, but Raven paid for it. This Izari had no money, as his pay was suspended after he was caught intoxicated in his office. He was still working in diminished capacity, but all of his pay went to his fine for two of their months.

"After he was deeply in debt to Raven, the supply of the little crystals was cut off until he agreed to take the nanobots," Wo concluded.

"Is this Izari still alive?" I probed.

"Probably. The Izari don't have a death penalty... for themselves, at least. He was censured and discharged from their military before the Izari destroyed your planet." Wo said.

I gave him a sharp look, "How did you know about that?"

"What I tell you now was told to me by Raven. It was a long time before the Izari found the nanobots missing. When they did, it didn't take long before they discovered the Izari responsible.

"Since he was recruited by Raven, they put a bounty on Raven while he was in the Market. He was found hiding in cargo bound for off-planet, arrested, and turned over to the Izari. They tortured him until he managed to escape back to the Thieves Market where he found me and offered me a huge sum to smuggle him back to Earth.

"We didn't even make it to your outer planets before the Izar ship overtook us. By the time we arrived at your moon base Raven was very ill, and your planet was destroyed. We landed at the base and the dock doors wouldn't open with his access code.

"By that time he was shaking badly, and then he went stiff and smelled of death. I dumped him outside for your people to find, and then I got the hells out of there," he finished.

The Raven was a fool. They had let him escape to lead them right back to the location of their stolen property. He should know that tactic, as it was a standard tactic in Special Services. Either he wasn't thinking clearly or he was only thinking of his own ass.

I only knew him by reputation, but that reputation was not for deeds you would discuss with anyone you wanted to remain your friends. He was assigned to black ops so deeply that no one would even admit that he existed, making conduct charges all but impossible. His death would be equally covert, remembered only for evil by a lone human and an exiled Prdynon. A fitting epitaph, for no one on Earth would ever know who brought death to the blue skies of their home.

Roused from my thoughts by a notification from the computer that we were approaching our destination.

"Do you know anything about the nanobots? How they work, any documentation, anything?" I asked.

Wo made a motion with his arms that I had come to learn was the equivalent of a human shaking their head. I know nothing about them. There was a memory crystal, though. Raven took it with the nanobots.

It would have logically gone to Mars with the nanobots, but why wasn't it in the memory core data that I had taken? This would require more thought at a later time.

I stood up, "Wo, if you will follow me to the bridge, we are almost at our rendezvous point."

XXI

Circling Oblivion

"Computer; Approach angle on forward viewer," I told the computer.

The image of space appeared in the concave screen that encircled the entire room. Directly ahead of us was a spherical asteroid about a mile wide rotating against the eternal night. To the left there was a void in the starscape. In the center of this void, a symbol indicated a black hole.

Wo's wings fluttered nervously.

"Computer; Analyze orbit of target asteroid."

A second later, the computer replied, "Orbiting at a distance of five hundred million kilometers. Orbital decay rate less than point one percent. Orbit estimated stable for approximately the next ten thousand years without external influence. Would you like asteroid analysis?"

"Yes."

"Asteroid is a sphere that is two point one-two-five kilometers in diameter. Rotational axis aligned with the black hole creating gyroscopic effect on asteroid," the calm voice said.

Wo spoke up, "I can't imagine how you can convey so much information from the limited noises you produce with your eating organ!"

I couldn't help but chuckle at that, "It will really blow you mind to know that we say even more without using our 'eating organ'!"

Wo suddenly looked panicked, "You are going to execute me?"

"No! It is a colloquialism meaning you will be 'very surprised'," I reassured him, "I will explain later!

"Computer; open short range comms, channel three-seven-one."

A beep signaled ready.

"Phantom to Banshee: Ready for entry," I said aloud.

"Banshee here, proceed to airlock," returned the familiar voice of Lobruc, "Was our endeavor successful?"

"Completely!" I replied.

The computer matched the rotational speed of the asteroid in a manoeuver that always made me dizzy. Slowly the asteroid appeared to stop in front of us, while the stars spun rapidly around us. The effect diminished as we approached a huge cavern in the side of the asteroid. A massive cog-like door rolled aside revealing an airlock several hundred meters deep. We passed through and the door rolled shut noiselessly in the vacuum.

The computer held the ship motionless in relation to its surroundings. The hull creaked and groaned as air began to exert pressure on her.

A short while later, the inner door rolled aside with a resonant rumble.

The Phantom emerged from the airlock into a huge void. When Lobruc had told me about his 'little place on a nearby rock' I was expecting a cargo pod anchored to an asteroid. This was far more than that.

"I am uploading landing procedure to your computer, Mac," came Lobruc's voice over the comms system.

The Phantom's computer showed the landing trajectory on the 3D display.

A few moments later, we were standing in just under one g of gravity. We felt motionless even though I knew we were still orbiting the oblivion of the black hole.

A doorway opened on a large habitat module and the stocky form of Lobruc appeared.

"Greetings, Mac! Is this our payday?" he asked.

"Bad news on that front, I'm afraid," I said as we walked into a large, elaborately furnished building.

A stunned expression spread across my face as I looked around. Lobruc's 'little place' was grand by any standard.

"Impressive place, Lobruc! The bounty hunting business must pay well in the Frontier," I said.

Lobruc would not be deterred, "Why is there bad news on our bounty?"

"The Izari think that they already have Wo. Another Prdynon 'borrowed' Wo's ship. The Izari pursued it and captured the other bug," I explained.

"So we can explain that they have the wrong bug…" he began.

"Without them discovering we helped him escape in the first place?" I interjected. "What did you do to get the whole station in an uproar? I was expecting a distraction, not a level one evacuation!"

"I started a fight between two races who have a long standing feud. It wasn't difficult, as they constantly look for reasons to kick the shit out of each other," he replied.

I chuckled, "How'd you do it?"

I slipped a tablet of Resht extract in one of the Hununi's drink. You probably don't know the following two facts, but they are very important! Number one, Resht only grows on Roalik. Number two, when administered to someone from Hunun, Resht causes their face to swell and turn green. It's harmless… unless they think it was a prank by their archenemies, the Roalikis. Then you have the result seen today!" Lobruc explained between bursts of laughter. "Every zig in the place was there and they couldn't separate them!"

Wo had been standing quietly just inside the door, wondering what these two aliens were going to do to him. He walked over to where we were, and cocked his head to one side. "I seem to be at your mercy at the moment. I am without a home or a hive, and I would like to know if I am to be killed?"

"To be honest, Wo, I didn't expect you to rendezvous with me. I figured you would make your escape when you took Azivdeo's ship! So you even being here is unexpected." I looked at Lobruc, "I have the information I needed. He has no bounty now, so as far as I am concerned, Wo, you are a free bug!"

Lobruc nodded his assent, "With no bounty, it wouldn't be worth my trouble to shoot him."

I smiled. "So what are you going to do with yourself?" I asked as we all walked toward a casual seating area.

I looked down at the furniture. It was little bigger than child size to me.

Lobruc gestured, "Just touch it, mammal."

I curiously probed the chair with my finger and it transformed to a much larger overstuffed easy chair! Wo touched another chair and it transformed into an inclined bench affair, with ledges along the side for Wo's extra legs.

"How did it do that?" I asked with unhidden amazement.

Wo said, "I know. Everything in here is a hologram with the exception of the three of us and the power plant and holo generators behind that wall. The computer just analyzed our anatomy and figured out where we bend."

I looked around in wonderment at the wooden beams, the elaborate furniture, and marbled floors, "Everything in here?"

"How did you know so quickly, Mr. Wo?" asked Lobruc.

Wo stroked his antennae nonchalantly, "I can see from infrared to ultra-violet. The force fields which make the projections solid appear translucent to me."

"You are correct. The generation equipment is the only thing real here apart from my food stores in a nearby cavern," Lobruc explained, "I keep the food in a chamber open to space vacuum. Excellent for preservation!"

"This is remarkable technology," I commented. "How long does the power plant last without refueling?"

"It's a radioactive decay unit with a half-life of two hundred years," he said.

This opened up another ten-minute conversation working out the time conversion between Sooggao Uxi and Earth, resulting in my conclusion that the power pack would have a half-life of one hundred and sixty Earth years.

"You impress easily, Mac. This is rather basic technology in most places," Wo said.

Lobruc left the room to get meals for us. Wo and I moved to the dining room and sat on chairs that also transformed to suit us.

A few minutes later Lobruc returned with three packages and a large bottle of liquid.

"Mac, you drink alcohol I recall," he said, "Wenvin Wo, is it acceptable to you?"

Wo looked pained as he fluttered his wings, "Please do not address me as Wenvin. I am no longer of that hive. I am merely Wo. Alcohol is poisonous to me. Water will be fine."

Lobruc paused and licked his eye, "My apologies. I too know the sting of rejection. I will get water for you, Mr. Wo."

"I am still shaken from the events of this day. Forgive my detachment. My friends and family sell me to be killed, and my enemy saves my life at great risk and for no reward. It's like everything I have been told since I was a grub was a lie," Wo chirped quietly. "I owe you both my life. This, I will not forget."

The high voice of Lobruc broke the solemnity of the moment, "Enough of this! We are three brave adventurers about to feast on this deep frozen bounty, not a trio of egg-layers digging a nest! Wo, you are both welcome to stay here as long as you need. Mac, do you need refuge for a while as well?"

I nodded, "That would be most welcome at the moment, Lobruc. Thank you for your hospitality. I was worried that you might be a bit upset at the loss of the reward."

"I do not go hungry, my friend. The gods have blessed me with success more often than failure," he explained, "so how can I be angry with them for keeping balance in the universe? You will both stay here! Now let's eat!"

*****

After the meal, Lobruc took us on a tour of his asteroid.

The first steps out of the habitat felt like walking outside on a cold, cloudy winter's night. We could only see the area that was illuminated around the habitat.

"How did you come to acquire this place, Lobruc?" I inquired.

Lobruc stood silently with his hand raised.

"How did you come to acquire this place, Lobruc?" my disembodied voice intoned again from the darkness.

Looking up with interest, I yelled "Hello!" once again.   One, two, three, I counted the seconds. As ten was approaching a distinct "Hello!" once again reached our ears. My battle computer told me the space was almost a mile in diameter.

"You can never be alone in here!", observed Lobruc.

"What is this place?" I asked.

He began, "This was a mining operation hundreds of years ago. These rock bubbles form when the black hole's gravity rips apart planets and stars. When a massive body explodes, gasses within the planet sometimes escape as a bubble of liquid rock. Occasionally one of these is blown into orbit around the black hole.

"Minerals crystalize on the inside as the orb cools. The inner layers are rich in many desirable substances.

"The Botreiki have been mining this part of the galaxy for thousands of years, and have this down to an art."

My mind was imagining planetoid sized geodes being flung into orbit by the death throes of its parent planet.

"How do they do it?" Wo asked. "I have dealt with the end result of their efforts for a long time but know little about where it comes from."

Lobruc continued, "First they select asteroids that are far enough out to nudge into a stable orbit. They then apply sufficient rotation to stabilize the orbit and generate gravity to make the extraction easier and faster. Then they cut the mineral layer down to the stone crust. The plasma laser cutting method seals the micro fractures in the stone making an airtight sphere as they go.

"They tried once to sell them to colonists to terraform the interior, but the few suckers who bought in discovered that the realities of life without sunlight wasn't something they were prepared to endure.

"Since then, they are simply abandoned and forgotten. Since they always orbit black holes, the one thing that every ship avoids, they offer exquisite privacy," he concluded.

"What about the machinery? Did they leave the air generators and airlock mechanism?" I inquired.

"There was no atmosphere before. When I moved here, it was just a hollow ball with a hole in it. I lived in my ship for a long time, until I found a good price on a used habitat.

"It was free actually. They are often abandoned or scrapped when the colonies build their permanent town. The tricky part is getting it back.

Most of the habitable planets in the Frontier are already colonized, so you have to go out a really long way to get them. It's almost to the point of being cheaper to buy new than to retrieve the free ones."

"I got this one about three hundred light years away toward the center of the galaxy. The planets are younger there, and complex life hasn't evolved on very many of them," Lobruc said.

"What about the airlock?" I queried.

"I had that made by the Kree," he said, "I hired a fitting gang to install it."

"That had to be an expensive project!" I commented.

"It was. For the first few years, I had to use a pressure suit to get from my ship to the habitat. It made keeping the ship in good repair a difficult task. That's when I decided to pressurize the whole place!" he said proudly.

I had to admit that I was impressed. This was an ideal base of operations for anyone who wanted to avoid leaving tracks.

Pirates were sometimes known to live permanently on their ships. That was an option if you had a large enough crew, and had the money to keep the machine alive.

Being able to land within an atmosphere made servicing a ship many times easier. This prodded me to open a possibility that I had been considering for a while.

"Wo, Lobruc, fate seems to have brought us together," I began, "and we must ask ourselves if we want to continue our journey together, or is this just one of the passing events in our lives which we will never forget? I think we are stronger together. Lobruc you are a known bounty hunter. You can be our public face. Wo and I are non-people, as we are both presumed dead. Wo is a talented thief, and espionage specialist, and I am... was, a deep cover assassin, and mission specialist. You have to admit that it forms a potent union."

Wo suggested we discuss it further inside before he went into hibernation in the cold outside the habitat.

A few minutes later and a few degrees warmer, we continued our discussion.

"I have been contemplating the same thing," said Lobruc lightheartedly, "Lobruc Intelligence Service has a nice sound to it!"

Wo made a gesture with his arms wide, "I will go with my new friends! I will not fail you!"

In a more serious tone Lobruc asked, "You were an assassin?"

After a deep breath I said, "Sometimes. I did many things for my government. A Special Services Field Agent had virtually unlimited freedom as to method, as long as the mission was accomplished. Sometimes a death was necessary to complete the mission… sometimes death was the mission," I told them solemnly.

A short buzz of the wings preceded Wo, "Before this day, I had never killed. That Prdynon was one of my own brood mates. While he had committed many crimes, none of them justified the terrible fate I thrust on him. If this is how you feel about the lives you have extinguished, then you have my sympathy."

I suddenly found myself saying things to these strange aliens that I had never said to anyone, "I got numb to it after a while. ' If I don't do it someone else will' you tell yourself. Then it becomes trying to quantify how many lives were saved by blood on your hands. It remains with you. Surrounding you like a shell that keeps everyone at a distance. I guess that's part of the reason I'm out here so far from my home."

"Were there many survivors?" Wo asked.

"Less than fifty thousand," I grimly replied.

"Something happened to Volkswagen?" Lobruc questioned.

That simple question broke the tension for me, and I laughed aloud.

"I'm afraid I was not honest with you on the elevator, Lobruc. I didn't know if I could trust you so I gave you fictitious information," I confessed. "Volkswagen was a brand of transportation device on my planet."

Lobruc produced his soprano laugh again, "A quick wit is the best tool a bounty hunter can have! Sooggao Uxi really means animal shit in my language!"

"Really?" I exclaimed.

"No!" he replied, "but you believed for a moment, so we're even!"

It felt strange to me to be building a friendship with these two aliens that wasn't solely to attain the goals of someone in some obscure office that I had never met.

I smiled, "We're even, Lobruc. We're even!"

"So what is the name of your planet, and what happened to it?" Lobruc asked.

"Earth. We were attacked by the Izari. I didn't know it at the time, but someone in the government acquired some Izar technology through sinister means. Our friend Wo here was the means," I elaborated.

Wo shuffled nervously, "I did not know what the liquid was. Nor did I know how the Izari would react!"

"I don't blame you, Wo. The agent you were dealing with would have found another way if you had turned him down. I doubt that the truth of who headed this operation will ever be known.

"When the Izari came, they didn't make contact with us. No demands, nothing. They just came in and destroyed," I told them sadly.

"It is a terrible thing," said Lobruc, "What was taken from the Izari?"

Wo stirred again, "My race too, was cast off our planet, many centuries ago."

"What was the liquid?" Lobruc asked.

"Nanobots.   Sub-microscopic machines. Some elements on my planet were trying to create enhanced super-soldiers. They had no idea just how spectacular their failure would be on this occasion.

"Too many scientists will simply take what they are given and build on it without questioning how the item was acquired. This insulates them psychologically from the blood that was spilled to get it," I explained.

"That problem," said Lobruc, "is universal!"

"I agree, and the people affected by their mistakes never even knew why they were dying," Wo pointed out.

I sat back and rubbed my eyes, "It gets worse. I was infected with the nanobots during the attack. Without them, I would have never survived, but now I can't go back home without the risk of infecting the remainder of my people.

"That's the whole reason I'm out here. I have to find a way to remove, or deactivate them... something! Hell, an owner's manual would help!" I told my companions.

Wo fluttered his wings excitedly, "I think I can help you. There are many Prdynons employed on Izar in servile positions. One of these Prdynons is a friend of mine. I used to sell some of his 'fortunate finds' in my shop. His family works for the Izari in question. That is how we were able to contact him initially. My friend, Voefsee Idi, is of another hive, so I should be able to contact him without danger."

"I stand ready to engage in another adventure! Oh, and to help my new friend!" Lobruc stated enthusiastically.

After a bit of thought I acquiesced. "It is a place to start! But I have no way to compensate you for this, not at this time anyway."

"Are we not starting a bounty hunting company? I propose the first article of our charter be that employees are entitled to complementary espionage services," said Lobruc as he stood.

Wo raised an arm, "I agree, and by majority it is approved. When do we leave?"

I laughed, "I've never seen individuals more eager to find trouble than you two!" I paused and gave them a solemn look, "Thank you both."

Lobruc beamed, "Without adventure, life has no meaning!"

Wo buzzed in agreement.

XXII

Answers Within Reach

"OK Wo, you know the target better than either of us, so what should we do?" I asked as I poured a round of drinks from a bottle of red liquid that my battle computer had identified earlier as alcohol.

The large insect wiped an antenna with one of his arms as he spoke, "I think it would be bad for you to be seen there. Prdynons are common. There are a few off-worlders seen on Izar, but not many.

"It's not considered a tourist spot, due to the arrogance of the Izari. They like to think of themselves as an ancient race. Old, and powerful they are, but they are not one of the Ancient Races."

I interrupted, "What are the Ancient Races?"

Lobruc answered, "The Ancient Ones are the few races who have survived from the first burst of life in the universe. They come and go as they please. They can manipulate time and space so that their ships simply appear where they want to be. They conduct their business and vanish. We are infant races to them, and they treat us as such."

"I have heard legends that told of one of the Ancient Ones erasing an entire race from history. They went backward in time and destroyed their home world before the first life ever developed. Their crime was testing a weapon that could trigger a star to go nova. They considered it a threat to the galaxy," Wo added.

"Gods," I said.

"Yes," said Lobruc, "Gods to many primitive worlds. Their symbols can be seen in many primitive cultures and in relics throughout the galaxy. Historians on my planet believe that the old gods on our planet were one of the Ancient Races, and there could be millions of other worlds as well."

Wo continued, "The Izari are a very old race, but they haven't quite evolved to the level of the Ancients. They have been known to intervene in interplanetary wars at the behest of the Ancients. Wars that were spilling over into neighboring systems. Their intervention usually consisted of decimating both sides, destroying every last trace of technological capacity. Effectively leaving both worlds in a primitive, pre-spaceflight condition, while leaving enough survivors to repopulate the planet. To give the race a second chance, if you will."

"That is precisely what they did to Earth, and we weren't at war with anyone!" I snapped.

Wo chirped a reply, "It seems strange that they did not seek the return of their property, they just blew their nanos up along with the inhabitants of the planets."

I agreed, "It didn't make sense to me either. Destroying a planet doesn't seem like a fitting punishment for theft on any world."

Wo pressed on, "Because of this extended relationship with the Ancient Races, the Izari think they are gods themselves. That works against them beautifully when you play upon their arrogance. They refused to believe that one of their researchers could be compromised by inferior beings with primitive thinking abilities."

"What was the drug that the Raven gave him?" I questioned.

"I do not know. It looked like broken glass," he replied.

Damn. That pompous son-of-a-bitch Raven had used an old Earth method that has been in disrepute for over a century to coerce the Izari to do his bidding. It was crystallized methamphetamine. It had fallen into disrepute in the 21st century when it was discovered that it was designed to be introduced into hostile populations, both foreign and domestic, as a method of control. Enemy soldiers lost their sense of fear and would charge directly into fire. When introduce into poor neighborhoods the drug caused crime, destruction and death, but it kept the populace in check. People who are afraid to open their door aren't likely to be protesting in the streets against those in power.

Trying to use this method against advanced races was stupid beyond belief, and when discovered bound to trigger retaliation. Worse yet, there was no way to know what effects this dangerous drug could have on other species.

I nodded slowly, "I know what it was, and I have bad news for him, there's no more where he got his last fix. If Izari reactions to this chemical are the same as human, he will go psychotic if he's a heavy user and can get no more. Time is short. Wo, can you contact your friend on Izar and get all the information you can?"

Wo rose and started for his ship, "I will contact him now."

I turned to Lobruc, "Have you had any dealings with the Izari?"

Lobruc licked an eye and said, "I have not been to Izar, but I have collected several bounties from them. They aren't very friendly, but they pay promptly with no bureaucracy."

"What are they like? As a species, I mean."

"They are an amphibian species. Their planet is almost all swamp, with few large bodies of water."

"What do they look like?" I asked.

Lobruc stood and crossed the room and retrieved a tablet display. He tapped it a few times and handed it to me and my battle computer translated and converted it.

The Izari pictured had a face reminiscent of a salamander. A thin grey skin failed to hide a network of blue-purple veins covering the bipedal creature. Their average height was listed at over two meters. Juveniles had tails, but lost them by adulthood. Lifespan unknown, but estimated to be three hundred plus Earth years.

"That's quite a database you have there!" I remarked as I handed the display back to him.

"I obtained it in payment from a Vajhi delegation," Lobruc said.

"Bounty?"

"No, the Vajhi are strictly nonviolent. They find it extremely distasteful. When they travel to certain areas, they would be a target for crime if they were unprotected. It's easy money, but the hard part is kicking the shit out of an attacker in a 'kind and caring' way!" he joked. "It has data on nearly every space-capable race in the galaxy, but it nothing on you Earthians."

I smiled, "We call ourselves humans, or scientifically, homo sapiens. We are a relatively new space faring race in the galaxy. We only made first contact with an alien race seventy-five Earth years ago, or about half of a human lifetime. That's all it took to mess up so bad that the race has been returned to living in caves and mud huts."

Lobruc nodded, "Believe it or not my friend, some haven't made it nearly that long. I have heard legends of a race which started an interstellar war between six star systems within five of their years."

"What happened to them?"

"That's the legend part. They were erased by the one of the Ancient Races after they found them to be a destabilizing race," Lobruc replied.

"You always speak of legends. Do you believe they really exist?" I queried.

His answer was instant, "Yes. I have seen their ships. They use trans-dimensional technology that the best scientists in the Frontier can't even begin to understand. It's almost as if they can bend reality to their will. I cannot explain it."

"Are they in the species guide?"

"No," Lobruc said as he poured another round of the red liquor. "They are very careful to limit their influence on lower life forms."

I shook my head, "It doesn't sound like 'limiting your influence' to erase planets from existence regardless of the crimes of a few."

"No one really knows what their motivation is. Plenty of people have their own opinion, but none is based on any hard facts. They seem to care for the galaxy as if it were a garden. Pruning here and there, eradicating the pests, and promoting the beneficial organisms."

"The only way to understand a man's motives is to be that man. Without a lot more information about them, there is little chance of building a coherent picture of them. Is it just one race which interacts here?" I probed.

"Legends say there are thirteen races remaining from the birth of life in the galaxy. There are many that are millions of years old, but the Ancient Races are some of the very few that outlived their home star," Lobruc said as Wo came back inside and returned to his unusual seat.

"I was successful in my effort to contact Voefsee Idi," said Wo, "The Izari we are interested in is taking a 'Meditative Sabbatical", this, my friend told me, was their label for house arrest and quarantine. He is not permitted to leave his home until certified by their Fitness Council, and no other Izari is permitted to enter. Pycari, the Izari, is delusional. Their doctors can't find the reason for his sudden bizarre blood chemistry, so he has been isolated to either recover or die. Idi is still allowed access to care for him because in the Izari view, Prdynons are disposable were they to become 'infected'."

I stood, "I think we can work with this data! Gentlemen, let's visit Izar!"

*****

Izar was a hot and humid world, as one would expect from a global swamp. There was only one large city built on ground drained sufficiently to support the buildings.

Pycari's home was well away from the city. He lived on a broad forested plain where low huts peeked out from behind native vegetation on mounds protruding from deep marshes.

Lobruc had been cleared quickly for planetary access, as he was familiar to them. Once we had been at low altitude Wo's stealth shuttle was released from the cargo hold. Wo dipped below the tree line for the brief instant it took me to dive into the murky waters and then returned to the hold.

I quickly surfaced and scanned the area. Even in the near absolute darkness, I could see as clearly as in daylight thanks to the nanos. Making my way silently toward the spot on the virtual map that hovered invisibly in front of my eye, a red number began flashing in the corner of the display. This planet was very hot, and my stealth suit was insulated for cold dark places. It was obvious that I wouldn't be able to stay here for very long.

After inspecting Pycari's dwelling, I found its connection to their power grid. One silent motion and a device from my pocket was attached to the circuits.

I returned to watch the front door. An insectoid form approached on the boardwalk and scurried up to the door.

He chirped quietly to himself. "I must be crazy for doing this. Wo owes me big for this one! Where is this mammal I am supposed to meet?"

"Closer than you think," I said from a low branch on a tree.

"Great Gods!" he exclaimed, "You scared the oils out of me!"

"Sorry. Open the door and there will be a convenient power failure in a few seconds. We will be gone before anyone can respond to the outage. No one will ever know I was here," I whispered.

Idi dipped his antennae in a fashion that I had learned was the equivalent of my nodding. He walked up to the access panel beside the doorway. A green light illuminated his face briefly, then a keypad appeared on the display. The door slid open when Idi completed the correct key sequence. He had just stepped inside when I triggered the device I had left on the power feed. The device responded by changing its properties from insulator to super conductor sending a back feed into the grid sending the whole area into blackness.

Idi waited just inside the door as I went inside to find Pycari.

He was curled into a tight ball in the corner, licking one eye and then the other continuously. I pressed an injector to the side of his neck and delivered a dose of a strong stimulant. It wouldn't be a substitute for what he had been on, but it might bring him around to coherence.

Slowly he began to blink and unwind himself. He tried to stand but collapsed back to the floor, trembling uncontrollably. The meth had had a devastating effect on Pycari.

"Pycari, can you hear me?" I asked looking into his eyes.

"Raven? Is that you, Raven? I need some more of the medication. Please, I am dying without it!" the emaciated form hissed.

"I am not the Raven. I do not have more of the medication. The place it comes from was destroyed by your people," I told him.

"No! No, Gods no! I didn't mean for this to happen!" he wailed. "Our elders were terrified of what the Lebrith would do if they found out their technology had been stolen."

His mind seemed to be clearing slightly but his physical withdrawal symptoms were severe.

"Tell me about the nanobots. How do you control them? Can they be removed from a host?" I questioned him.

The Izari shuddered and vomited. "We do not know how they work. They use trans-dimensional technologies from the Ancient Lebrith. We were given them to inject into our global reactor. It was failing and threatened the whole planet. The nanobots repaired and upgraded the reactor from the molecular level, inside out."

Pycari shuddered once again and lost consciousness. I injected him again with a larger dose of the stimulant.

"I need to know how the nanobots are controlled, and can you remove them from a host?" I demanded.

"I do not understand what you mean. They stay in the reactor forever running autonomously. We never control them. They use a sub-quantum processor that exists in several dimensions at once. They see what needs to be done and do it..." he cut himself off with a scream of pain.

At that moment, I heard the chirp of Idi from the door. "Some Izari are coming! You must go!"

A tap on my battle computer signaled Lobruc to make another pass for pickup.

Pycari grabbed my arm as I turned to leave, "Please don't leave me this way!"

Hesitating for a moment, I pulled a thin, glasslike quill out of a container from my suit and handed it to him. "This is quick and painless. Just insert it into the skin, death will come," I said solemnly to the pathetic creature.

"Thank you," he hissed as I exited the hut.

Two Izari patrolmen were already on the walk to this hut. I leapt out in the darkness and grabbed the same branch I had used awaiting Idi, who was now locked in the hut's toilet.

A sudden noise emanated from the tree branch as it bent under my weight.

"What was that!" hissed one of the patrols as they swung their light up just in time to see a featureless shadow disappear into the canopy.

"Stop or we fire!" came through the heavy air half a second before a barrage of plasma fire.

I felt myself falling before I felt the pain of the shot that burned into my right shoulder blade. Plunging deep into the warm waters, I disappeared from sight. Dizziness overcame me from the pain and shock of the wound.

I groped around with my left hand trying to find something to orient myself by. In a few feet, my groping hand found a piling, and I pulled myself underneath the boardwalk with the nanobots supplying my cells with oxygen. I followed it away from the voices I could hear above, searching for my body.

After a few minutes, the pain had subsided significantly, but my right arm was still useless. I moved the edge of the boardwalk taking care to stay below the water, as I watched a display count down the seconds until Wo's ship would be over me.

Typing with my nose, I sent Wo a short message: Hurt. Land.

A single word appeared in reply, "Understood."

Seconds later Wo's stealth shuttle glided silently in until thrusters were needed to hover over the marsh.

I sprang out of the water onto the boardwalk and lunged for the nearby open door trying to beat the inevitable plasma fire. Searing bolts of hot plasma passed me, with a few impacting on the ship. The hatch closed as I dived through. Consciousness faded as I felt the tug of inertia as we accelerated away with more questions than we arrived with.

Epilogue

Kvaaa'tu's musical voice sounded, rousing me from my narrative. The translator's lights flashed furiously before it spoke.

"Kvaaa'tu closes the file on Earth, but wishes to continue documenting MacKesson's unusual circumstance. MacKesson will be compensated in a manner to be agreed upon at next data acquisition meeting in four cycles, if MacKesson finds the proposition acceptable," said the translator.

"MacKesson accepts. I will return here in four cycles," I said.

Kvaaa'tu proffered a memory crystal in his thin hand. As I accepted it, the translator said that it was a transcript of our meetings for my records.

Realization dawned on me of the possible value of these records for mankind when they again reach for the stars. Maybe they will be able to use them as a roadmap to avoid the pitfalls, which claim so many young races.

I stood and faced Kvaaa'tu, "Thank you for the copy."

Kvaaa'tu raised a hand and gave his departure greeting as I headed to the Phantom and back out among the stars.